CONFESSIONS
OF AN
APOSTATE

This is a volume in the
Arno Press collection

THE AMERICAN
CATHOLIC TRADITION

Advisory Editor
Jay P. Dolan

Editorial Board
Paul Messbarger
Michael Novak

See last pages of this volume
for a complete list of titles.

Confessions

OF

AN APOSTATE

[Mary Anne] Sadlier

ARNO PRESS
A New York Times Company
New York • 1978

Editorial Supervision: JOSEPH CELLINI

———•———

Reprint Edition 1978 by Arno Press Inc.

THE AMERICAN CATHOLIC TRADITION
ISBN for complete set: 0-405-10810-9
See last pages of this volume for titles.

Manufactured in the United States of America

———•———

Library of Congress Cataloging in Publication Data

Sadlier, Mary Anne Madden, 1820-1903.
    Confessions of an apostate.

    (The American Catholic tradition)
    Reprint of the 1903 ed. published by P. J. Kenedy,
New York.
    I. Title. II. Series.
PZ3.S127Con 1978   [PS2749.S37]   813'.3 77-11308
ISBN 0-405-10850-8

1864

Confessions

Of An

Apostate.

PEASE

BY MRS. J. SADLIER.

Confessions

OF

AN APOSTATE.

By Mrs. J. SADLIER,

AUTHORESS OF

"LIFE IN GALWAY," "BESSY CONWAY," "ELINOR PRESTON,"
"THE CONFEDERATE CHIEFTAINS," "HERMIT OF THE
ROCK," "CON. O'REGAN," ETC.

NEW YORK:
P. J. KENEDY,
PUBLISHER TO THE HOLY SEE,
EXCELSIOR CATHOLIC PUBLISHING HOUSE,
5 BARCLAY STREET.
1903.

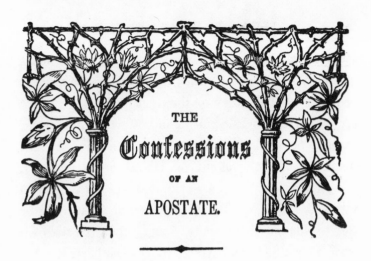

THE
Confessions
OF AN
APOSTATE.

OME years ago the people in that part of the beautiful county of Wicklow which adjoins tne Vale of Glendalough were puzzled by the appearance of an aged man who suddenly took up his abode in a cottage between Laragh Bridge and the Valley. This cottage had been for years and years inhabited only by an old woman and her grandson, a bright boy of twelve or fourteen. The house had been a snug little farmhouse, but for many years past decay had been making sad inroads on its once snowy walls, and the

kitchen was the only part of it in use, that being
quite sufficient for the accommodation of the humble
occupants. The story of the deserted cottage is but
too common in Ireland. The widow of its former
owner, being unable to pay the advanced rent
demanded by the agent of her absentee landlord,
was turned out on the world, and her farm thrown
into a sheep-walk. For years after, no one could be
got to inhabit the cottage, fearing that the widow's
curse might be in and around it. At last it received as
a tenant old Milly Nolan, whose youth and middle age
had been passed in the service of the agent's family.
As no one else would live in the cottage, Milly was
permitted to take shelter in its mouldering walls with
her then infant grandson, whose father, her son, had
been a soldier and died abroad. The poor boy's
mother had died in giving birth to little Tony, so
that the child was solely dependent on his aged relative. Milly contrived " to keep the life in them," as
she used to say, herself, " by showin' the Churches
an' things to the quality from abroad that came to
see the sights in the glen within." Tony, too, being,
as we intimated before, a smart, active lad, was soon
able to do a little business on his own account in the
cicerone department. His extreme youth, coupled
with his natural quickness and that precocious humor

which distinguished him from all his brother or sister guides, made him exceedingly popular with all tour- ists, so that "Little Tony" was more in demand, by the time he was twelve years old, than any other "guide" about the Seven Churches. Hardly a day went over his head—at least during the summer months—that he did not bring home some silver pieces to his granny, and his exultation knew no bounds when the querulous old woman used to say in a tone of surprise that was not quite free from vexation:

"Why, then, bad cess to you for a *sprissaun*, where in the wide world do you get all the money you do? I'm sure I don't know how it is that you always get more from the quality than any one else!"

One fine summer morning when the brown moun- tains and the dark glen were looking their best, and the world outside was all joy and sunshine, the old man already mentioned alighted from a jaunting-car at Milly's door, much to Milly's surprise, for Milly "had never laid eyes on the decent man before," and the car-boy told her he had driven him from Round- wood where he staid over night "at the head-inn, no less." So Milly could only drop a low courtesey, and offer a seat to the stranger, with a "God save you, sir," while Tony, drawing back into a corner, took a

eisurely survey of the " sosh ould gintleman," whose
sun-burnt face told of a protracted sojourn in foreign
climes. The car-boy, to the full as curious as either
of the others, having thrown his horse a handful of
hay from the well* of the car, took up his station
half in and half out the doorway, with his shoulder
resting against the post, so as to see and hear what
was going on between " Milly the Glen" and the
strange traveller from foreign parts.

Great was the astonishment of the three listeners
when the old gentleman asked Milly if she could rent
him a room. " Humph !" said the car-boy to himself,
" he's no great shakes after all, when it's here he'd
hang up his hat," and he glanced contemptuously
round on the half-ruinous walls of the little dwelling.
" He's not right *at* himself," was Milly's first thought.
" He's a queer customer, I'll go bail," was Tony's
more correct idea.

Milly's apprehensions with regard to the old man's
senses were very considerably lessened by his handsome offer for the use of the little room and her
general services, and by the time he had taken out a

* To those who have never seen that peculiarly Irish convey-
ance a jaunting-car, it will be necessary to explain that the *well*
is the middle portion of the vehicle, bounded on either side by
the back rails.

sovereign and placed it in her hand as "earnest," she would have taken her book-oath, if anybody asked her, that "there wasn't a thing the matter with him—barrin' the outlandish look he had, an' the quare old face for all the world like a *leprachaun* or something that-a-way."

All Milly's excuses about the miserable condition of the place were thrown away on the stranger, who appeared to take no notice of them whatsoever. When he had seen his baggage, consisting of two trunks, safely lodged in the best of the two rooms, he got on the car again, and telling the wondering car-boy to drive him back to Roundwood, away the car jingled, leaving Milly and her grandson to rub their eyes and get over their astonishment as best they could. Toward evening the car rattled back again, bringing the stranger and some necessaries for his new *ménage*. Soon after a carman arrived with a bed and bedding, and some other few articles of furniture, and it took Milly and Tony all the evening to put things to rights by bed-time, the old man having walked abroad after supper and left the house to themselves.

"By dad, Tony, agra! this is great luck for us," observed Milly, "but what in the world brings him here, do you think?"

Tony's shrewdness was altogether at fault—"he couldn't make head or tail of it." "But did you see how he went about the house, granny? just as if he had been in it all his days!"

"Wisha, then, Tony, I noticed that myself, an' the way he looked about him, too, with the tears in his poor ould eyes—do you know what came into my head, Tony?"

Of course Tony did not know, whereupon his granny vouchsafed graciously to enlighten him. "Only it's easy to see that the ould gintleman comes from beyond seas, I'd be most sure that this wasn't the first time for him to be here——"

"Whist, granny! here he comes!"

How far correct Milly was in her shrewd surmise the sequel will tell, but however that might be the stranger soon made himself quite at home in the neighborhood. Although he frequently took Tony for a companion in his rambles, it was evidently more for the pleasure of his company than from any need of his guidance. Before Tony had gone with him many times, he told his granny in confidence that "the ould gintleman knew every foot of the place as well as he did. Sorra bit but he could find his way with his eyes shut." Milly heard this with a gleeful chuckle, as it went to confirm her own opinion

"An' as for the Saint," went on Tony, "why, he knows all about him, granny. There isn't a guide about the Seven Churches could hould a candle to him. Whiles I think he must be a fairy, Lord save us! for you'd swear he was to the fore in the Saint's own time."

"Wisha, then, Tony avick! but you make my flesh creep, so you do!—an' how does he say he came by so much knowledge as he has?"

"Why, he says he got most of it out of books, but, *inagh!* they'd be the quare books that 'id tell him all *he* knows! I'll tell you what it is, granny, I'm gettin' afeard of him—I don't half like the way he gropes about among the graves, and, listen hither, granny!" The boy drew down his grandmother's head, till he whispered in her ear: "when he goes in, at times, to the graveyard, he makes *me* wait outside till he comes back—either that or sends me off home. Isn't that quare?"

An exulting laugh was Milly's answer. "Not a bit quare, Tony agra! it's jist as I tould you at first —there's some of his people in it, an' he doesn't want *you* to see what grave he goes to. Watch him now, an' you'll see if I'm not right."

Tony watched accordingly, and from his perch on the churchyard wall behind a tall elm, he saw the mysterious old man kneeling by a neglected grave in a remote corner, his tears falling fast and thick on the long grass. There was nothing ghostly about this—it was real human sorrow, and it went to Tony's heart. From that day forward he attached himself to the stranger, and followed him in all his wanderings as a faithful dog follows the footsteps of a kind master. And kind the stranger was to Tony, whose affection he quickly saw and appreciated. He seemed pleased to have the boy with him, and loved to draw out his quaint, old-fashioned drollery by encouraging him to talk without reserve. They were an oddly matched pair, drawn together by some invisible link which it would puzzle the most astute metaphysician to define.

The sudden appearance of the stranger, and the seclusion in which he lived, gave rise to many strange reports, and for some time he was persecuted with inquiries, both public and private, as to who and what he was, and whence he came. The professional services of Milly and her grandson were in greater request than they had ever been, but the public curiosity seemed to be transferred for the time from St. Kevin and his traditionary miracles to "the mysterious hermit," as the ladies, especially, loved to call our unknown   It was seldom, however, that they managed " to get their eyes on him," for once he found out that he was the greatest *lion* of the place, he studiously kept out of the way during visiting hours. His ingenuity was, it is true, put to the stretch, for parties of curious ladies, and not less curious gentlemen, arrived at all hours under pretense of seeing the Valley at sunrise, at noon, at sunset— or by moonlight, as the case might be. Some of the night arrivals, being told, in answer to their whispered inquiry, that the old man was in bed, insisted on Milly's making some excuse to open the door that they might get even a distant glimpse of him. The request being backed by a piece of silver, Milly's fidelity was put to the proof, and she seemed half inclined to yield, but Tony indignantly made answer that they wouldn't disturb the gentleman for all the money in Dublin town.

" Well, well, Tony! I b'lieve you're right," said Milly, "I know if he woke up on us, we'd be kilt entirely." Further expostulation was useless, so the disappointed tourists went off in a pout, declaring that they'd never set foot in the Valley again, nor sixpence of their money Milly should ever handle.

Next morning Milly took the first opportunity of relating what had passed over night; the old man heard her with a smile, till she wound up with : " It's well come up with them, indeed, to be goin' on their *tower*, drest up like any quality! It's little bother ' the sights' 'id give them, I'm thinkin', if it wasn't for their ould lad of a father that turned for a wife, an' got an elegant fine house an' a power o' money with her. The dirty drop is in them, if they were hangin' in diamonds!"

"Mind your own business, woman!" said the stranger with sudden emotion, and rising from the table, he left his hardly-tasted breakfast, and calling Tony to follow him as soon as he had broken his fast, rushed out of the cottage, leaving its inmates to make what comments they pleased on his strange and unaccountable emotion.

When Tony, with a whack of oaten bread in his hand, overtook him, a few minutes after, on the road to the Churches, he could hardly get a word out of him. They entered the dreary Valley, and there the old man, seating himself on a stone by the road-side, fixed his eyes on his wondering attendant who stood silently before him looking at everything but him. "Tony!" said the old man. "Well, sir!" "I'm going to give you an advice that will be better to you than silver or gold!"

"I'm very thankful to you, sir!" said little Tony.

"Never give up your religion, Tony! no matter what comes or goes, *keep it* hard an' fast!"

"Is it to turn my coat, you mane, sir?" said Tony half indignantly. "Ah, then, with God's help, there's little danger o' that anyhow!"

The stranger shook his head. "Don't be too sure of that, Tony, my man! I've seen some in my time that were as steadfast as ever you could be—ay! till they were man-big, and yet, Tony! the world and the devil got the better of them—yes, my boy! and they sold themselves body and soul for—pshaw! no matter what!"

A party of tourists were now seen descending the steep path from St. Kevin's Bed, and the old man left the Valley precipitately, muttering to himself: "If the half of them staid at home and minded their business 'twould answer them better. This is no place for idle curiosity, and it's not one in a hundred of them that has any other motive in coming here."

A year or two of this kind of life seemed to soothe the stranger's troubled mind, and in the practice of religious duty, with such works of charity as presented themselves in that secluded spot, his days rolled on in peace. The only one whom he visited was the parish priest, and with him many of his hours were spent. Many attempts, direct and indi-

2*

rect, were made to get at his history through the
priest—for people had all made up their minds that
his reverence knew all about it—but pumping and
sounding, and all the other ingenious contrivances
failed. If Father O'Byrne knew the secret, he kept
it to himself.

It was not till the old man's death, which occurred
about two years after his arrival in the neighborhood,
that his story was made public, and then by his own
request, in order, as he said, to deter others from
treading that path which he had found so fatal. The
following is that portion of his autobiography left in
the hands of the priest for publication. It may be
well to mention that little Tony was not forgotten.
Twenty good pounds were left him by his old master,
quite enough "to make a man of him," as old Milly
said, but it didn't make a man of him, for Tony was
still "Little Tony, the guide-boy," and for many and
many a long year after his twenty sovereigns lay
snugly away in company with some pounds of silver,
in Milly's "old stocking" somewhere up in the thatch
over the house-door.

THE CONFESSIONS OF AN APOSTATE;

OR,

LEAVES FROM A TROUBLED LIFE.

THE term *apostate* is a harsh one to apply to one's self, and I must confess I do not half like the look of it when I have it down in black and white. Truth must be told, however, and I know very well that long before my story is ended the Catholic reader will have no qualms about the application of the word, so I may as well anticipate the verdict.

How I came to fall away from the faith of my ancestors is at times a marvel to myself, although when I have traced the course of my apostasy, my readers will find it all so natural as to excite no surprise in them. The same causes have, doubtless, produced, and will again produce, the same effects in those who voluntarily thrust themselves into temptation, when far away from the healthful influences and the salutary restraints that made their home-life virtuous and happy. For their benefit, then, I will do violence to my proud heart and tear open the festering wounds which Time, the great healer, has partially closed.

My childhood and youth were passed amid scenes calculated to nourish piety by raising the mind from earth to heaven I was born in Wicklow County, in the immediate neighborhood of Glendalough, "the Irish Palmyra," as it has been aptly called. The particular "spot where I was born" is of little consequence to the reader ; suffice it, then, to say that it was about midway between Laragh Bridge and the entrance to the Valley, somewhat nearer the latter. My father was a small farmer, rather easy in his circumstances, inasmuch as he was always able to face the landlord on quarter-day, and was, moreover, the owner of considerable stock, principally consisting of those goats whose milk converted into " whey " is a favorite specific for incipient consumption among the inhabitants of the Irish metropolis. The scant herbage of those mountains is peculiarly palatable to the hardy animal whose presence alone gives life to many a desert-scene in that wild, remote region. Many of my childish days were passed following the goats over and around the mountains which encircle the gloomy vale, and it was my pleasure to clamber after my sure-footed companions to the highest steep of Derrybawn or Lugduff, and thence look down on the wondrous scene beneath and around me. The gloom of St. Kevin's Valley was awful to me, and

when, at times, I did venture down amid the mouldering relics of the past with which it is so thickly
strewn, the silence and utter loneliness of the place
chilled my young heart. And yet I loved dearly to
tread my way amongst the old tombstones, half-buried
in the grass, and creep under the crumbling arches
at the apparent risk of being crushed beneath some
falling fragment. The danger, however, was only
imaginary, as I soon found out. The masonry at
Glendalough is proof against time and the elements,
as grey and seemingly as indestructible as the dark
rocks around.   Much of it will stand in all probability
to the judgment-day, like the faith which reared
those sacred piles in the infant days of the Irish
Church.

As a general thing, however, the children of the
neighboring district have no fondness for the Glen.
The everlasting gloom which rests upon it, owing, I
believe, to the dark coloring of the steep mountains
around—the silence that broods within it "from night
till morn, from morn till dewy eve,"—the air of solemn
mystery which overhangs the ruins, with the weird
and lonely pillar-tower rising like a tall spectre high
over all—oh! it is a scene of more than desert solitude, and its desolation is oppressive even to persons
of mature age.

Some of my very earliest recollections are of devotional assemblies in the old stone-roofed chapel known to our antiquarians as St. Kevin's Kitchen. Its wonderful state of preservation induced some former parish priest to make use of it as a chapel of ease, for the convenience of the surrounding peasantry, and during all the years of my youth it was our general place of worship. It was there my mother took me by the hand on Sunday and holiday mornings to hear Mass, followed by a colloquial discourse from his reverence Father Brannigan, the most paternal and the best-natured of all old priests. It was there we children assembled again in the afternoon for Catechism, and I can well remember the various traditional anecdotes of the great St. Kevin and his successors in the Abbacy of Glendalough, wherewith his reverence used to diversify his familiar instructions. It was in that lone mountain-chapel, amid the mouldering bones of many generations, close by the silent city of the dead that I, with a brother and sister, made my first Communion, and the simple joy of our parents is even now vividly before me, although forty-and-three years have passed since that auspicious day, and the snow of a premature old age has settled on my head.

When a few more years had rolled away I began

occasionally to make my " stations," that is to say, to perform at a certain spot within the consecrated vale, a certain numbers of prayers and penitential works, cheering my drooping spirits ever and anon with thoughts of the superhuman endurance with which St. Kevin and many other holy men had there undergone all manner of austere self-punishment and mortification. So great was my fervor then that I wished I had lived when Glendalough was a city and the old Abbey and the Seven Churches were all frequented by saints, who spent much of their time in prayer and penance. Many a time I made my mother laugh by wishing with a heavy sigh that I could be a Saint. I often wished her to tell me what the Saints used to do, but my poor mother, although well acquainted with the popular tradition of the place, was not much versed in hagiology, and from her I learned passing little of the real every-day life of the holy anchorets around whose desert retreat a city had sprung into existence. She told me to ask Father Brannigan, but I never found courage to do so.

At a later period of my life I learned more about the past of what I might call my native Valley than any of my immediate progenitors had ever dreamed of in their pastoral simplicity. Looking back on that religious solitude with the light of history and of

antiquarian lore, it has a character of supernatural
sublimity, and over it hangs a cloud of mystery
which enhances its solemn and gloomy grandeur.
As I gamboled with my brothers and sisters,
and other pupils of the hedge-school, kept within a
bow-shot of the Glen's mouth by the self-esteemed
philomath Patricius O'Grady, none of us ever thought
of St. Lawrence O'Toole, when Abbot of Glendalough, going out in the dead of night to that very
graveyard to pray for the souls of the generations
who slept beneath. Even had we known it we could
not then have appreciated the strong faith and the
tender charity which moved the soul of the holy
Abbot during those mystic communings with the
Master of Life and Death amongst the mournful
dwellings of the dead. Still, even with the knowledge I had then, I reverenced the Saints in general,
but especially the great St. Kevin of Glendalough,
whom I considered as holding a very important post
in the court of heaven.

My recollections of the Valley are not all of a
sombre or religious kind. Once a year, during the
merry month of May, the people flocked thither from
all the surrounding parishes to celebrate the patronal
feast ; and then, at least, the old walls and the lake
shore and all the lonesome Glen resounded with

shouts of harmless merriment and light-hearted glee.
It was a sort of carnival for the whole country-side,
and it seemed as though every soul of the laughing,
frolicsome crowd went there with the fixed intention
of making the Glen as noisy and as full of life for
that one day, as it was silent and lugubrious all the
year round.

It was, on the whole, a joyous and a stirring scene,
and were it in any other place but the Valley of
Glendalough I could look back on it with unalloyed
pleasure. As it is, with the more correct taste aris-
ing from some degree of cultivation, I cannot bear
to dwell on " the patron," because it jars on my
recollections of the silent and holy Glen, just as I
would shrink from disturbing the stilly surface of its
dark waters where the grey old ruins have been
mirrored from time immemorial. Taking one thing
with another, my peasant life near Glendalough was
both innocent and happy; but it passed away all too
soon, and left me alone and unsheltered in a new,
and, alas! a far more trying phase of my existence.

When I was about sixteen, my father died; and
although my eldest brother was come to man's estate,
and had been for years the chief manager of our
little farm, still the head of the house was gone, and
the family began to scatter. One or two of the boys,

3

younger than I, took it into their heads to learn trades, and my mother did not wish to prevent them, although it made her heart ache to see any of us leaving the paternal cottage, and worse still, passing from under the maternal care. My eldest sister was sent to keep house for an uncle whose wife had died; and another went "to serve her time to a manty-maker," as the all-important fraternity of dress-makers are styled by the Irish peasantry, in utter disregard of etymological propriety. For myself, I all at once discovered that herding goats on the mountains was not my vocation, and the ruins of Glendalough had no longer the same attractions for my newly-awakened spirit. The lough's "gloomy shore" might be a very pleasant moonlight ramble for the troubled ghost of the fair Kathleen, but to me it became a very dull, common-place sort of thing, and I even began to laugh at the time-honored traditions wherewith tourists are successively entertained, for which contumacious heterodoxy I got "my head in my fist" sundry times from the wrathful "guides," the Hades of those scenes.

At heart, however, I still reverenced the sanctity of the place, and I never could pass any of the Seven Churches or the old Abbey-walls without a feeling of religious awe. This was strengthened, unconsciously

to myself, by a tradition which I have since found
common to all, or nearly all, the ecclesiastical ruins
of Ireland, but which I then only knew in connection
with our own Valley. It was one of those which I
earliest heard, and it took, of all others, the deepest
hold on my imagination. The legend went that in
old, old times, no one knew how long ago, a certain
graceless wight who had spent his Saturday night
and Sunday morning in a shebeen-house, up somewhere amongst the mountains, was taking a short-cut
home through the Glen at the very hour when Mass
was going on in the chapels all the country round.
All at once the sonorous chime of a church-bell broke
on his ear, and turning round in a fright, what should
he see but a priest saying Mass in the old Teampul na-
Skellig, where there was no roof but the blue sky,
and hardly enough of the walls remaining to shelter
a banshee. It was a ghastly sight for mortal eye to
look on, for the priest was not of this world, nor yet
the cowled monks who formed his congregation.
Spectres they all were, sent to warn the unhappy
reprobate, as he well knew, of the tremendous value
of the Holy Sacrifice. Tradition says that the lesson
was not lost on the careless sinner who, from that
time forward, was careless no more, and never after
neglected the command to sanctify the Sabbath at

east by hearing Mass. Let no one scoff at this simple legend, for in it lies a profound meaning, and it is such traditions that help to keep the faith alive, and ever burning in the hearts of a Christian people. Well for me and many, many others, if we had never been drifted by the current of life out of the reach of these moorings. Many of those who bear the brand of *Apostate*, will echo these words with a sad and heavy heart. But now for my " ower true tale."

CHAPTER II.

SIMON GOES TO PUSH HIS FORTUNE.

IME rolled on—one year followed another, and I was fast approaching the age of manhood, without the smallest prospect of any change in my condition. Day after day I toiled away on my mother's little farm, always looking dreamily out for some lucky chance of bettering my fortune, and at the same time seeing the world. I was naturally of a romantic turn of mind, and although the world of romance had scarcely ever been presented to my view through the medium of books, still I was not without my inspiration. I had drank in with greedy ears the stories which old people told around the winter's hearth of venturesome poor boys like myself—most of them rejoicing in the name of

3*

Jack—who had left their natal cot "to go and push their fortune." Success had invariably crowned the search—so that fortune was sure to be found by those who sought her in earnest. Although I could not expect to fall in with any enchanted princess who, rescued by my puissant valor, would reward me with her fair hand, and the trifling compensation of "a crown of gold," or any of those beneficent fairies who brought about such happy results in that indefinite period "once upon a time," still there was wealth to be won, and honors, too, in that world which I pictured to myself in such glowing tints. To go no farther than Dublin "there abroad," had not Timothy Scanlan, a neighbor boy of our own, made a power of money in it, and all in the course of a few years, as everybody knew? Inflamed by the recollection of Timothy's success, I waxed more impatient from day to day, saying to myself, as I rested on my spade in the potato-garden behind the house, "Now, Simon, my boy, if people can do so well in Dublin, what must it be in foreign parts? I'll go bail, it isn't plantin' potatoes you'd be, if you onst got there. You'd be a gintleman in no time, Simy dear, with a fine shuit o' clothes on your back, an' a watch in your fob, too—who knows?" And thereupon I dashed my spade into the ground with renewed vigor. " Work away now, Simy," I further soliloquized, " your diggin' days 'ill soon be over, please God! Ah! but what will the poor mother do then?"   This thought smote heavily on my heart, and I began to whistle "Paudeen O'Rafferty" at a furious rate, in order to drown reflection for that time.

My poor mother did not fail to notice the change in my habits.   Indeed, my very appearance changed, for the struggle perpetually going on within me, between ambition and the newly-awakened desire of " seeing the world" on the one hand, and my filial and fraternal affections on the other, gave me neither rest nor peace.   I grew pale, thin and languid, and my mother began to fear that there was something the matter with me.   Many a milk-posset, and savory little messes not a few, were prepared by her kind motherly hands to tempt my failing appetite, but still she had the mortification of seeing me dull and heavy, and, with a view to divert me, she one day told me to take " a slip of a pig " she had, to the market town a few miles off, and sell it.   I went accordingly, but, as my mother often said, in after times, " it was the dear journey to her."   At the market I met an old acquaintance of ours, one Patt Byrne, who had some years before removed to

another part of the country. Patt was very glad to
see me, and, of course, I was just as glad to see
him. I had disposed of my "*boneen*" to good advantage, and, that care off my mind, I was nothing
loath to accept the treat which Patt insisted on giving me for the sake of "Auld lang syne." While
we sat in a back room, in Johnny McGrath's public-
house, sipping our respective glasses of "the real
mountain-dew that never seen water," we discoursed
of many things, chiefly relating to my poor father,
who had been a bosom-crony of Patt Byrne's long
before my advent, and long after it, too. All at cnce
however, Patt threw me into an awful flurry by the
announcement that he was going with his family to
America.

"To America!" I cried out in surprise, "ah then,
Patt, what put that in your head?"

"Why, then, bad cess to the one o' me knows,
Simy, barrin' it's a letter I got from Tommy Smith,
the boy that my sister Catty ran away with a little
before we left your neighborhood."

"Well! an' how did he do?" I inquired with
breathless interest.

"How did he do, is it? why, I b'lieve he hardly
knows the end of his own riches—that's how he
done."

" An' you're all goin' to where he is ?"

" By dad, I b'lieve so. My woman has got the notion in her head, an' I'm not much again it myself either, for we have a family growin' up, you see, an there's no prospect here for them but hard work an' little for it."

" I'll tell you what, Patt !" said I starting to my feet; " I'll be with you myself, if God spares me !"

" You will, Simy ? why, then, I pray God it may be a good move for all of us. You'll be able to do more for the ould woman there than you would here, twice over."

It was then agreed that I should break the matter to my mother with as little delay as possible, and, her consent once gained, proceed with my preparations as fast as I could, for, as Patt said, " a good thing couldn't be done too soon."

We parted on these terms, and, as may be believed, I lost no time in asking my mother's consent to my going. It was no easy matter to obtain it, not even so easy as I expected. In vain did I hold out every inducement that I could think of. All was no use, or some time. The mother's love was too powerful to be overcome by reasoning, or by any amount of promise.

" Now, mother dear !" I said on one occasion when

I was almost in despair, "you know if I stay here for fifty years we'll be no better than we are now, an' I never can do anything for you like what I'd wish to do. If you'll only let me go, now, you'll see the fine baver bonnet I'll be sendin' you some o' these days all the way from America—an', may be, a shuit of silk into the bargain!"

This brought a smile to my mother's wan face, but she shook her head resolutely. "Don't be tryin' to palaver me that way, now, Simy! you know well enough I wouldn't wear silk no matter who sent it, for that's what no one belongin' to me ever wore."

But although promises relating to herself were all thrown away, my mother could not hold out against my continual entreaties, backed by those of my brothers and sisters, who thought it would be a fine thing to have one of the family, at least, on the high road to fortune. She was obliged to give in at last, and as we had no ready money in our possession after paying the "May gale," she told me with a faltering voice to take off one of our three cows that she named to the next fair, and see if she wouldn't bring enough to pay my passage and rig me out for the voyage. The blessing which I invoked on my mother at that moment was so fervent and so full of feeling that it brought the tears to her aged eyes.

I was too much elated then to heed her emotion, but I have many a time thought of it since those loving eyes were closed for ever.

So the "fine springer" was sold, and, to my great joy, a fine price she brought. My sea-stor was amply provided, including a number of cakes of double-baked oaten bread of my mother's own making—she would suffer no one to have a hand in it but herself. A voyage to America was then far different from what it is now, and was considered a sort of neck-or-nothing enterprise, that was either to terminate in an ocean-grave or a fabulous amount of wealth. It was looked upon as something awful to "tempt the great deep," and he who made up his mind to undertake the voyage was regarded with a sort of romantic interest, not more on account of the positive dangers he was about to brave, than the mysterious regions to which he was going and the strange adventures which were supposed to await him—adventures, however, which were all to "lead men on to fortune." My mother's consent once gained, there was little else thought of, or little else done in the house for the intervening time but "getin' Simy's things ready." To the younger members of the fami'y there was pleasure in the bustle of preparation, altlcugh their labor of love was not

unmixed with sorrow ; but for my poor mother there
was no joy—no amount of hope could cheer *her*.
For myself, I kept out of her sight as much as I
possibly could, for her grief touched my heart to its
very core, and I feared that my resolution might give
way, if I allowed myself to think of her approaching
bereavement.

It is needless to dwell on the final parting. Such
scenes are too painful to be often exposed to the
public eye,—an organ which is usually more critical
than compassionate. Suffice it to say, that about the
middle of June, just when the whole country round
was preparing for St Kevin's " patron," Patt Byrne's
family and myself, with a couple of neighbor boys,
who had been incited to follow my example, all set
out for Dublin, accompanied for miles and miles of
the way by a numerous " convoy " of friends and
acquaintances. When it came to the last, my heart
almost failed me, and it required all the courage I
could muster to sustain me at that trying moment.
But even that passed away, as all things earthly do.
My poor sorrowing mother, and all the rest of my
kindred vanished from my eyes—alas ! that I should
say, for ever. There was no time to look about me in
the great city, for the ship in which our passage was
taken was to sail in an hour, and we were obliged to

hurry at once on board, and leave all the city wonders unseen—those wonders of which we had heard so much.

Our voyage was rather tedious, and its vicissitudes were many, including perhaps, more than the usual amount of sea-sickness   Patt Byrne lost his youngest child, a rosy, chubby, prattling boy of three years old ; and the event threw a damp on us all, especially when we saw the poor little fellow, who had been a general favorite in the steerage, sewed up in a canvas and thrown overboard.   That was the first cloud that settled on our path, and I have often thought since that it was ominous of evil.   Its impression on us youngsters was, however, only transient, and when, at the end of nine dreary weeks, we were told by the sailors that we were on the far-famed "Banks of Newfoundland," we were " entirely elevated," as poor old Patricius O'Grady of erudite memory used to say.   Boston was our destination, and when, after a few days more, our ship cast anchor in Massachusetts Bay, and we saw the stately old Puritan city before us, with its numerous spires and its palace-like dwellings, rising grandly from the bosom of the waters, we forgot all our sorrows and all our troubles, and felt that " all sorts of good luck " must await us in that land which presented to our view so noble a frontispiece.

4

The captain of our ship had taken a fancy to me
at an early period of our voyage, and he was good
enough to interest himself on my behalf. He pro-
cured me a situation as porter in an extensive hard
ware establishment, the proprietor of which was an
old friend of his. My enthusiastic admiration of
" America " had been somewhat staggered by the
state of affairs in the marine lodging-house where
we had all " put up " for the first week. It was one
of those old, rickety wooden buildings much beloved
by bugs, and other such nocturnal vampires which
are unluckily no rarity in seaport cities ; and as those
interesting insects are well-known to delight in
" alien " blood, I was so tormented that I almost
wished myself back again in the old whitewashed
cottage among the bare Wicklow mountains, which
humble dwelling was, at least, bug-less. The temptation to repent was happily of short duration. One
of the other porters at Brown & Steenson's, hearing
of my affliction, kindly undertook to procure me
relief, laughing heartily the while at my piteous complaints, and telling me for my comfort that that was
little to what I had before me. His laughter annoyed
me a little at the time, but I soon forgave him, for he
made arrangements that very evening for me in his
own boarding-house, where I next day made my

entrance, very glad to get rid of my first lodging by paying for the week I had but just commenced. The change was a positive relief to me, for, although it was no more than a third or fourth class boarding-house, still it was clean and well kept; and I felt, as I stretched my weary limbs for the first time on the soft flock bed, that there, at least, I was sure of obtaining that rest which for many nights I had wooed in vain. And I was not disappointed. Sleep settled, like a halcyon, on my heavy eye-lids. I slept and dreamed of home—

" The home of my fathers—that welcomed me back."

That home had not yet lost its charms for me. The old affections that bound me to its inmates were still strong, and fresh, and active. I did not repent coming to America, for my path had been, as yet, smooth and easy ; and I was just at the age when novelty has charms that can give enchantment to all we see There were some things, however, that even novelty could not make agreeable. Of this kind was the peculiar manner in which every one spoke of Catholics, those of Ireland in particular. I soon found out that most of my fellow-boarders, some eight or ten in numbler, were *not* Catholics, whatever else they might be. From their conversation I gathered,

to my utter dismay, that to be a Catholic was bad
enough, but to be an Irishman and a Catholic reduced
a man to the very lowest social grade. My good
natured comrade, who was himself an Englishman,
seeing my confusion, and the mortification which I
could not conceal, took up the cudgels on my behalf,
and told the others flatly that " he didn't see but
what Hirishmen were about as good as other men,
and if most of them *were* given to Papistry, and fond
of counting over beads and such like 'armless fal-de-
rals, why, no one need quarrel with them for that.   It
didn't do no one any 'arm but themselves."

An ironical " hear, hear !" from various parts of
the room greeted this blunt, but well-meant declaration. My friend, no whit disconcerted, laid his brawny
hand on my shoulder, and went on :

" Them's my notions, now, I tell you plainly ; and
another thing I have to say is this : You know as
well as I do that this 'ere lad is from Paddy's land.
It ain't manly, then, to be eternally down on th
Hirish when they're only as one to ten in the house.
I won't stand it no how, for it was I brought him
here, and I'll see that he gets fair play while he's
in it."

There was some grumbling on this, and not a few
sarcastic observations on this newly-awakened sym-

pathy for the Irish, but my friend was not a man to be trifled with. Like that prince of recruits who was met by "Sergeant Snap at the fair of Clogheen,"

> " His brawny shoulders *were* four feet square,
> His cheeks like thumping red potatoes,
> His legs would make a chairman's chair "—

he was, in short, a burly, stout young Englishman, strongly imbued with that love of fair play for which his countrymen individually (not nationally) are distinguished. It so happened that most of the other boarders were but sparely gifted with personal strength or vigor, and the stalwart proportions of the "man of Kent," inspired them with considerable respect, not altogether unmixed with fear. As a general thing John Parkinson was the best-natured soul living, but occasions did sometimes turn up when he expressed himself with an energy that startled his hearers, and gave them the idea of a lion waking up from sleep and shaking his shaggy mane with a threatening growl. The present occasion was one of these, and hence it was that when he enforced his last words by striking the table with his fist, at the same time casting a glance of fierce inquiry around the company, the sneer vanished from every lip, and each one tried to give the affair the appearance of a jest.

4*

" Jest, indeed !" said John, " there's no one likes a
jest better than I do, but I can't stand such jests as
that, no how ! Let the lad alone, that's my advice to
you all !"

Next time we were alone together, I expressed my
obligations to Parkinson for his friendly interference
in my favor, but honest John interrupted me with :

" Don't mention it, Simon, don't mention it, if you
please ! If the Pope himself was in your place, John
Parkinson wouldn't be the man to stand by and see
him crowed down that way—though most like I
wouldn't stay long in the one house with him—but,
howsomever, Simon, I go in for fair play, and that's
an advice I'll give *you*,—always take part with the
weakest, be they right or be they wrong ! Lend a
hand here to hoist this bale !"

" What is that, if you please ?"

" Don't be making a fool of yourself showing off
Popery airs. That sort of thing won't go down
here, take my word for it. It was all very well in *your*
country where the people were most all of one way
of thinking, and where you could walk on your bare
knees from morning till night without no one laughing at you ; but here the people's all wide awake,
Simon, and you'll have to be wide awake, too, if you
want to get along. If you keep your Popish notions

to yourself, and don't let any one know what persua sion you belong to, you'll go ahead fast.   Mind your business, Simon, and let religion alone—pack it off to your old mother in Ireland, my fine fellow !"

There were some things in this speech that I found it hard to swallow, especially the contemptuous allu sion to the " Stations," which I had been taught to regard with so much reverence.   But when I looked at John's frank, good-natured face, and saw the benevolent smile with which he regarded me, I couldn't for my life resent that or anything else he had said.   So I merely thanked him for his good advice, and promised to make no unnecessary display of religion for the time to come.

Notwithstanding the protecting kindness of John Parkinson, I could not help feeling a sense of loneli ness on finding myself alone amongst Protestants, a state of things which had never entered into my calculations.   I had never before come in contact with any but those of my own religion, and it seemed so strange to hear the holiest things, the most sacred mysteries, spoken lightly of—it was so startling to find people doubting and scoffing at truths which were to me as certain as my existence, that I felt bewildered as one rudely awoke from a dreamless slumber.

I was mistaken, however, in supposing mysel the only Catholic in the house. There was one young fellow whom I had all along taken for a North of Ireland Protestant, notwithstanding his Milesian cognomen of O'Hanlon. He was a thin-faced, sharp-featured young man, with that shrewd and reserved cast of countenance which usually belongs to our Gaelic kinsmen of "Auld Scotia." He had never taken part in any of the conversations concerning religion, and seemed, as I thought, perfectly indifferent about the matter.

Who can imagine my surprise when, on the first Thursday after my arrival, Harry O'Hanlon overtook me as I was returning to the store after breakfast, and accosted me with:

"I say, O'Hare, what are you going to do to-morrow?"

"Do to-morrow! what do you mean?"

"Why in regard to eating meat—you know to-morrow's Friday!"

"I know it is—but—but—why, to be sure I can't eat flesh-meat, any how!"

I fully expected to see O'Hanlon burst out laughing, but he did no such thing.

"All right, Simon, that's just what I wanted—now, I'm a Catholic, too—"

" You a Catholic! the sorra that you are now, O'Hanlon! simple as you think me, you'll not put that down my throat."

" Well, believe it or not, I tell you I *am* a Catholic, though, God help me! I'm only a poor one—but let that pass for we're both in a hurry. The old dame never puts a bit of fish on the table on a Friday or Saturday, and, till now, as I was the only Catholic in it, I hadn't the face to ask her for any."

" And what in the world did you do?" I interrupted.

" Well, God forgive me," he said with some embarrassment, " I done what many a one like me has to do here—when I couldn't get fish, I eat flesh!"

" The de'il's in your gut then!" I exclaimed indignantly, " aren't you the nice fellow all out?"

O'Hanlon laughed good-humoredly at what he called my childish anger. " But keep your temper, now, Simon, till you hear me out. Now that there's two of us, we can ask for fish with a better grace, and *eat* it too, if we get it, which I wouldn't have cared to do before. What I want you to do now, is to back me up when I ask Mrs. Johnson to have fish cooked for us two on Fridays and Saturdays.* If

* It will be remembered that this was forty-eight years ago, when meat was forbidden on Saturday as well as on Friday.

she refuses, we'll both threaten to leave, and then she'll give in, I know, for the house is rather thin with her at the present time."

Of course I promised to do my part, and, wondering what was to come next in so queer a place—at least amongst such queer people—I went to resume my work.

CHAPTER III.

MRS. JOHNSON was quite as surprised as I had been when O'Hanlan, with no small degree of hesitation, preferred his request that he and I might have fish for our Friday's dinner. The chopping-knife wherewith she had been doing her best to pulverize some roast beef for that peculiarly American compound known as "hash," suddenly suspended its operations; and she stood looking from one to the other of us with a comical look of bewilderment. Catholics, the reader will remember, were but sparely scattered in those days amongst the people of the Puritan city. The veritable " follower of Rome " was almost as great a curiosity as a Choctaw or a Cherokee.

" So you're a Papist, after all !" said the wonder-ing Mrs. Johnson ; " well, I never ! and you want fis on Friday now, though you've been eating meat here every day for over half a year. What's got into you now, Mr. O'Hanlon ?"

O'Hanlon explained that so long as he was alone, he didn't care to trouble her to provide fish for him ; and, besides, he was rather afraid of the others laugh-ing at him. But now that he had another to back him up, he didn't mind—one of us would keep the other in countenance.

" Well ! I guess it's about the same thing to me," said Mrs. Johnson, resuming her chopping, " whether I cook fish or flesh for you. If you had only said the word before, I'd have given you fish as often as you liked. Some folks wouldn't give in to Romish super-stition like that ; but that ain't my way—I jest try to give my boarders whatever they like best, and, although I can't for my life see what difference it makes whether folks eat fish or flesh—if so be that it doesn't disagree with them—still, I go in for letting every one have his own way so long as he pays me for my trouble."

Satisfied with this we left the kitchen. As we

ascended the stairs we heard the old woman remarking to her "help," viz.: a stout New England girl who was her "maid of all work."

"Did you *ever* hear of such strange people as the Irish? I guess them and the Jews are most the same. The Jews won't eat pork, and the Papists won't eat fish—except at particular times. But I swon, I wouldn't have believed that Hanlon was a Papist. I suppose, now, it's because he's afraid of the other chap telling that man they call the Pope of Rome. I have heard tell as how if any one was accused of disobeying him, he'd send orders immediately to some of his secret agents, and before the poor unsuspicious victim could know anything about it, he'd be whished right off and clapped into a dungeon somewhere, and fed on bread and water no one knows how long!"

The girl's exclamation of horror came out in such fervor, that it was as much as O'Hanlon and myself could do to get out on the street before we gave free vent to our merriment.

"Why, then, now, O'Hanlon," said I, when he had closed the door after us, "do you think there's any one in America so simple as to give ear in earnest to such foolish stories as that?"

"Ay, indeed are there, Simon!" replied O'Hanlon,

5

still laughing at my earnestness. " There's thousands
and tens of thousands that are cute and sharp enough
in everything else, only in regard to Popery, as they
call it. The most nonsensical story any one can
invent about priests or nuns, or the Pope, or the like
o' that, oh, be dad ! it'll go down slick with them—I
have heard stories of the kind myself that would
make a cat laugh till she'd split her sides, and still it
was every word taken for gospel."

" Well, if that doesn't bate Banagher !" I exclaimed, " sure a weeny little child at home would
have more sense than all that comes to !"

" To be sure it would, Simon ; for there everybody
knows the differ, but here, you see, it's most all hear-
say with them, most of them knows as little about
Catholics as they do about the man in the moon, and
their preachers are the greatest hands in the world-
wide, by all accounts, at inventing stories—just like
the old *seanachies* that used to be goin' about long
ago in Ireland—they earn their living, the creatures !
by making stories and telling them. The only difference is, Simon, that the *seanachies* used to tell abou
ghosts and fairies, and the like, and the ministers
stories are all about Popery !"

Not much enlightened, but more mystified than
ever by O'Hanlon's explanation, I went off to Patt

Byrne's to see how things were getting on there. I
found the whole family in high spirits. Patt and his
eldest son were both employed by the corporation,
and between them they brought in twelve dollars
every Saturday night. Their work was hard, to be
sure, very hard, but what of that, they said, so long
as they were well paid for it. They evidently did
not calculate then, what sad experience taught them
afterwards, that twelve dollars a week in a large city
did not go far beyond the support of a large family.

"Why, Simy!" said my friend Patt, "if things
goes on in this way, it's buyin' property I'll be some of
these days—Nancy an' myself took a walk out a
Sunday evenin' to see some lots for buildin' that they
say are to be got very reasonable."

"Yis," put in Nancy, "and we're goin' to put up
a nice little house on the lot when we get it, and I
think we'll have a room to spare for you, Simy, and
then you'll come and board with us—won't you
now ?"

Of course I promised, nothing loath, and nothing
doubting, either, that out of such fine wages a "lot"
could soon be bought, and a house put up, too, and
all the rest of it. They were all much interested by
the account of my adventures at Mrs. Johnson's.
The delinquency of Harry O'Hanlon in regard to the

Fourth Commandment of the Church excited their warmest indignation, and all I could say in his favor afterwards was of no use. Patt declared energetically that he wouldn't trust his life in that fellow's hands—no he wouldn't. A man that wouldn't stand up for his religion, or do what it commanded him, because there happened to be odds against him, deserved to be whipped at a cart-tail, Patt said.

"But they tell me it's very common here," I observed in extenuation.

"Get out!" said Nancy with more zeal than politeness, "what sort of an excuse is that? I wish to the Lord some of them lads were at home in the ould country and do the likes of it—if it wouldn't be dear pickin' to them I'm not here. Why, they'd never get over the shame of it the longest day they'd have to live!"

But if they were severe on O'Hanlon's backsliding, my worthy friends were full of admiration for the generous liberality of John Parkinson, whom they expressively apostrophized as "the broth of a boy."

"And him an Englishman and a Prodestan'," said Patt, "and to take your part that way; well, now see that. I'll tell you what it is, Simy, you must bring that chap to see us some evening; I could divide my last mouthful with a fellow like him. Be-lad I could!"

"But where's Billy?" I said, looking round as I rose to go. This was their eldest son, whose absence I had not before noticed.

"Why, sure enough, we forgot to tell you," said the father, "the priest made us send him to a night-school, as he's at his work all day. There's one of the finest priests here, Simy, that ever stood at an altar. Nancy there was at Confession with him last Saturday was eight days, and she says he's a saint if there's one livin'. I mane to go myself a Saturday evenin' if God spares me, for his reverence sent me word by Nancy that he'd be ever so glad to see me. But what was I talking about—oh! the night-school —well! Billy's goin' every evenin'—barrin' Sunday —and you wouldn't b'lieve, Simy, how well he's gettin' on. His reverence said it was the pity of the world not to give him a chance of the larnin'."

This started a new idea in my head. If Billy Byrne, who was at much harder work than I, all day long, could go to a night-school, what was to hinder me from doing the same. A thirst for knowledge was one of my master-passions, and shared with am-bition the empire of my being. From my earliest boyhood I had been looking forward to some indefi-

5*

nite period when I could gain access to the fountai
of knowledge, and drink my fill of their myst*e
waters. If I ever was to rise in the world, I had an
idea that it must be by knowledge and skill, not by
labor. Here, then, was a golden opportunity held
out to me, and I grasped it with an eager hand.

Having ascertained from Patt where the school
was to be found, I went straight thither, and made
arrangements to commence my studies on the following evening. I had never thought of asking the
Byrnes what the master's religion was, but I soon
found out that it was just what it ought to be. The
teacher was a good, simple-hearted Kerry man,
wholly unskilled in the world's ways, but well versed
in classical and other lore, both ancient and modern.
He was a devout Christian, a *protege* of the excellent
priest of whom Patt Byrne had told me, and the
pedantry which formed his most striking characteristic was so very amusing, and at the same time so
very inoffensive, that you could not help liking the
old man even when he assumed the greatest sternness.
You felt that far down under that thick layer of
pedantry and that other thinner one of scholastic
exactness, there was a world of truthfulness and
genuine kindness, and that the quaint exterior of the
pedagogue covered a heart attuned to the softest

harmony. It was lucky for poor Philippus O'Sullivan, as he chose to call himself, that his pupils were
young men rather than boys. Had they been of an
age for flogging, I verily believe the old man would
have been the subject, they the masters, for his rule
was simply no rule at all. The doctrine of "moral
'suasion" was as yet unbroached in theory, but in
practice it was identically that which my old master
carried out in exemplary fidelity. Fortunately for
his credit—for I confess I have no faith whatever in
"moral force" as applied to urchins at school—he
was saved the necessity of keeping a day-school by a
certain little office which his kind patron had pro-
cured for him, and which occupied his time from nine
till four every day. With us of more mature growth
he was exceedingly popular, perhaps fully as much
on account of his grotesque *physique*, and the amusement we derived from his quaint, old-fashioned ways,
as the real good qualities which adorned his inner
nan.

It so happened that Master Philippus took quite a
fancy to my unworthy self, notwithstanding that I
played more tricks on him than any other in the
school. He saw that I was pursuing knowledge with
all the fervor of my heart, and as he used to say in
his own peculiar way · "It does me good to see a

well-endowed youth bending his head lovingly to
drink of the Parian spring spoken of by that true
and ever-to-be-remembered poet, Alexander Pope.
Surely I esteem myself highly favored when an all
bountiful Providence permits me to hold the cup—
that is to say, boys, to be made the humble instrument
in replenishing your young minds with the fullness
of that wisdom which proceeds not from books alone,
but also from a close observance of men and things
as we see them in this mundane sphere of ours—"

To what an extent poor Philippus had observed
" men," the foregoing remarks will show ; but as for
" things " he had certainly given them much attention, and was no mean authority in the physical and
exact sciences.   There was one thing—yes, there
were two things in which the old man excelled most
men whom I had as yet known.   These were inex-
tinguishable love for his native land, and a child-like
submission of his understanding to the teachings of
religion.   Like most Irishmen deserving of the name,
he cherished the memory of the old land as something inseparably connected with religion.   With
him, Ireland ought still to be the Island of Saints,
and the national reputation was, I think, dearer to
him than his own.   It was a strange lot that had
cast him over the great sea into the heart of that

foreign city; foreign indeed to him, forming a unit
in the great numerical whole, but as distinct in his
national and personal peculiarities as man could well
be. His very walk on the street when you chanced
—and it was a rare chance—to meet him abroad, told
you that he was merely *in* the community, not *of* it,
for while multitudes hurried past him to and fro,
intent on the visible world around them, he glided
like a spectre through their midst, looking strangely
grave in his long brown *surtout* closely buttoned to
the chin, little heeding the human vortex whirling
around him, but wrapt up in his own cogitations, and
journeying, it might be, on the top of Parnassus, or,
more likely still, through the storied passes of his
own mountains far away in " O'Sullivan's Country."
He was a man of the past, that old Philippus, yet he
was neither dry, nor cold, nor even insensible to the
boyish ambition which lured us on up the steep path
which leads to Science. Although caring little for
the world himself, and despising in his heart all i
has to offer, he certainly did his best to fit us, his
pupils, for the several parts by it assigned us.

Under Mr. O'Sullivan's tuition, I made considera-
ole progress in the several branches to which I ap
plied myself. By his advice I made grammar, arith-
metic, and book-keeping my principal studies. I soon

found my account in this, for Mr. Brown, my first employer, having himself taken the trouble to examine me, and being satisfied with my capacity, obtained for me a good situation as clerk in another hardware establishment. This was another step in advance, and it was with a proud and exulting heart that I sat down to inform my mother of my good fortune. I had written home regularly every few weeks since my arrival in America, and in the answers which I duly received (elaborately penned and indited by no less a person than Master O'Grady himself,) my poor mother never failed to express her satisfaction at the wonderful change that was taking place in the style and appearance of my letters. At first she could hardly believe that I wrote them myself, and the neighbors were all of the same notion, she said; but after a little, when I had really convinced both her and " the neighbors," her exultation knew no bounds. These letters from home gave much pleasure to Mr. O'Sullivan, whose kind heart rejoiced in the happiness which he felt was chiefly his own work; but unluckily Patricius O'Grady took it into his head to append to one of the long-winded epistles a postscript of self-laudation. He always knew, he said, that I'd come to something, for he gave me " what you might call a good foundation."

" I'd like to know what it was, then," said Philippus
testily, " I'm sure I had to dig it out, and lay every
stone of it myself. He lay a foundation, the block-
head ! That's what he'll never do, Simon, except it
may be a foundation of stirabout in his own paunch
Foundation, indeed !"

It required all the little address I was master of
to soothe the professional vanity of my worthy pre-
ceptor, disturbed and irritated by the assertion of a
rival claim on the part of the obscure O'Grady. I
could only succeed by a very unprincipled deprecia-
tion of the attainments of that personage, together
with an humble confession of the lamentable state of
ignorance from which Philippus had drawn me forth.
Many a good laugh O'Hanlon and I had over the
harmless oddity of the worthy pedagogue, and even
John Parkinson, bluff Englishman as he was, con-
ceived a real regard for " Old Phil," as we were wont
to call him.

I could laugh then at the droll peculiarities of the
good old man, but now I could weep to think that I
did not honor him as he deserved, and that I did not
imbibe some of that science which made him " wise
unto salvation," when I drank in so eagerly, and in
such copious draughts, that profane learning which,
compared with the other, and wanting it, is worse

than useless. But the past cannot now be recalled. My race of life is run, once for all, and the many false steps I made are never, never to be retrieved on earth.

During the year and a half that I remained at Mrs. Johnson's, O'Hanlon and I had many taunts and much ridicule to endure on the score of religion, and there were times when I almost wished that I was like the others, restrained by no ties of conscience from eating as I pleased at all times. It was hard, I used to think, that the Church should insist on that which made her children ridiculous in the eyes of others. Not that I felt it any privation to eat fish on Friday and Saturday—the good old custom was still " second nature," and I had no " yearning for the flesh-pots " of others. But I was painfully sensitive to the shafts of ridicule, even though despising those who launched them, and I never *could* get accustomed to the slang abuse so plentifully heaped on the religion I professed.

Each time that I went to confession, however, I got over this false shame for a few days, or perhaps a few weeks, but unfortunately it was only at Christmas and Easter that I went, and a specific applied at such long intervals could have little effect on the tenor of a life Occasionally, to be sure, when I

went to High Mass, I heard some discourse that
affected me for the time, and brought back a portion
of the old fervor that was as fast disappearing from
my mind and heart as the rustic bashfulness and boy
ish simplicity were from my outward bearing.   The
corduroy breeches and Caroline hat, which had formed
important items in my outfit, were long ago laid aside
as unfit for the *pavé* of Washington Street, and with
them went by degrees many of the minor observances
of religion, which, like them, I thought, were " too
Irish " for a polished state of society.   Still I was a
Catholic in form, and to some extent in feeling.   I
generally contrived to put in a word in defence of
my religion, too, whenever it was assailed in my presence, especially if the assailant was an intimate acquaintance, or if the odds were not against me.
Nothing would have hurt me more than to tell me
that I was growing cold and indifferent in religious
matters, or to hint that there was any possibility of
my falling away from the faith of my fathers.

Still I could not be insensible to the change that
was coming over me   When, for instance, I received
a letter from my mother (as all the family epistles
were written in her name), I no longer received her
maternal admonitions as I formerly, or even recently,
had done.   She would tell me in the inflated language

of O'Grady : "Son of my heart, I pray God night and morning that the dew of His holy grace may pour down its choicest blessings on you, and that your eyes may never go astray after the follies an vanities of that great city.   Every day you rise keep God before your eyes, and never forget your morning or evening prayers.   I hope you'll never leave off that blessed and holy scapular that I got you invested with before you went, and that you'll have the beads always about you, so as to keep you from all harm."

These pious and affectionate injunctions used to bring the tears to my eyes for the first few months after I came to Boston, but now I glanced them impatiently over, with a flushed cheek and a contemptuous curl of the lip.   "What a foolish old woman !" I muttered, half-ashamed to hear myself speak so of such a mother ; "it is hard to say whether herself or her amanuensis is the greatest fool !   Beads indeed !   I'd to see myself caught in Boston with a pair in my pocket.   If I followed *her* advice to the letter, I'd soon be an old *voteen* myself."

Nevertheless, I took care to send her some money from time to time, and my letters were more affectionate than one would suppose from the callous state of indifference into which I was rapidly sink

ing. I laughed to myself, notwithstanding, as I
thought of the

> "—— fine beavers and fine silken gowns"

which I had held out to my poor mother as an in
ducement.

"What a figure she'd cut in a silk dress, poor old
body!" I soliloquized; "sure it's drugget or stuff
that answers the like of *her!*" I forgot that my
new-fashioned mode of reasoning only brought me to
the same conclusion which my mother's good sense
had reached long before. Tranquil and content in
her humble sphere, vanity and ambition were strangers to her bosom; and when I, in my boyish folly,
lost sight of the fact, she rebuked me with all the
simple dignity of a true Christian. But at this time
I was wholly incapable of appreciating the nobility
of soul which raises the Christian above the puerile
vanities of this vain world.

About eighteen months after my arrival in Boston,
I was left in a minority of *one* in Mrs. Johnson's
domicile. Harry O'Hanlon saw fit to take to himself
a helpmate and "went house-keeping," to my great
discomfiture, for now I feared the scoffs and jeers of
my companions more, far more than I did at first.

While I was looking forward with the most gloomy

forebodings as to my future comfort in the nouse, an incident occurred which I could neither have foreseen nor expected, and which bettered my condition more than a little.

CHAPTER IV.

MRS. JOHNSON ISSUES A MANIFESTO

ONE Friday, a week or two after O'Han
lon's departure, one of our boarders,
a self-conceited young "down-easter,"
was, as usual, making merry at my expense in regard to my eating fish when
I might have flesh.

"I guess you'll find that mackerel
rayther salt," said he, "suppose now
you were to try this here roast beef
Can't, eh? Well! that's what I call
rayther hard. Why, man, the priest won't know
anything about it, except you tell him, and I reckon
you might leave *that* out when you go to confession
—eh, Kerrigan? *will* you be a man for once?"

"To the mischief with that rusty mackerel," cried

another, " I wouldn't touch it with the tongs. Mrs.
Johnson, it's all along of you this nonsense of Kerrigan's; if you didn't put fish on the table he'd have
to eat what he could get, and he'd thank you in the
end, even if it annoyed him some at first. He'l
ruin his constitution eating fish two days in the week
He will indeed."

Mrs. Johnson's grave countenance grew graver as
she replied : " I'd have you to know that I'll hear no
more of this. Let the young man eat what he has
a mind to. It ain't my way to meddle with such
things, and, besides, I don't know but what the Papists are right and other folks wrong."

We all opened our eyes wide and fixed them on
Mrs. Johnson's face, which looked rather blue at the
moment. One made an exclamation of surprise, another upset his " tumbler," and a third pushed back
his chair with such angry force that one would suppose inwardly vowing never to eat again. For me,
I could only gaze in speechless astonishment on the
face at the head of the table and the two grey eyes
that were peering curiously at us all through a pair of
shell-mounted spectacles.

" I say they *may* be right," repeated Mrs. Johnson
very slowly ; " I went last night to the Popish meeting-house, lown to Franklin street, to hear Bishop

Cheverus, and, my stars! 1 can't keep from thinking ever since of what I heard him say. He's a most uncommon wise man, and talks like a phophet—I think such words I never heard from the mouth of man, and I wouldn't believe, if any one swore it, tha a Popish priest could talk so. He was just a talking of folks fasting and denying themselves for Christ's sake, and I *tell* you, he did make me feel wonderful queer. So says I to myself, 'Rachel Johnson,' says I, 'if you choose to go right straight on yourself eating the nicest things you can git hold of, don't find fault any more with folks that are willing to deny themselves for conscience' sake—and that's jist what I mean to do, and I tell you I'll have no one at my table that *won't* do it. He's a most uncommon larned man that Bishop Cheverus, and I do believe that a man so good and so larned, cannot be wrong. So I mean to tell our minister next time I see him." Then addressing me she said, " Eat your dinner, Kerrigan. No one shall meddle with your choice so long as you eat at *my* table. I opinionate that Papists ain't half so bad after all as folks make them out. I said so to Deacon Lowe on our way home las night, and the Deacon said that that 'ere Bishop Cheverus *wasn't* a bad man, anyhow! for he had had his eye on him most all the time since he's bin in Bos-

ton, and if he ain't a real out-and-out good Christian
he never saw one—that's all he'd got to say."

The sneer had gradually vanished from every face
as the blunt, earnest old woman thus delivered herself. The whole city of Boston was at that time, as
or years and years before, lost in admiration of the
great and good man who had left his home and
friends in the sunny land of France to labor amongst
strangers in a foreign clime, and under sterner skies,
for the extension of Christ's Church. His virtues
were on every tongue. His talents and accomplish-
ments were the theme of general praise even amongst
the fastidious and " exclusive " *literati* of the self-
styled "Athens of America." Men and women of
all creeds, and of no creed, thronged to hear him
when he preached, and his resistless eloquence,
strengthened and enforced by the purity of his life
and the heroic virtues which all men can admire but
few imitate, made a lasting impression on his hearers.
Before his heaven-inspired reasoning the mists of
prejudice cleared away, and men who merely went
through curiosity to hear him were astounded to find
themselves believing as he did before they left his
presence. In him the majesty of religion, the dominion of virtue, were displayed to an incredulous world.
That world seeing, was convinced, and if all were

not converted, all were induced to think well of a religion which they had been taught to look upon as omething diabolical.*

The name of Bishop Cheverus, then, commanded the respect of the entire city, and the interest which every one felt in his affairs was truly remarkable. Even my messmates, indifferent as most of them were to all religion, had nothing to say against the good Bishop, and the mantle of his exalted reputation served to shield my unworthy self for the time to come, from the wanton attacks of my sportive persecutors. My abstaining from flesh-meat on any particular day for conscience' sake was something which they regarded as very funny, indeed, but when they heard of such abstinence being defended and justified by the great man whom all Boston looked upon as something beyond the ordinary race of mortals, it became quite a different thing, so that I never after had anything like the same amount of ridicule to encounter on that particular ordinance of religion.

The esteem in which I saw the good Bishop held —even by the Protestant community—was a subject

* In proof of this it may be mentioned, that, when this illus trious missionary was collecting funds to build the first Catholic Church ever put up in Boston, he was generously assisted by the wealthy Protestant inhabitants of that city.

of salutary reflection to me." "Now," said I to my self, "here am I almost ashamed of my religion on account of its being so different from others. I'm ashamed of going to confession, and try all I can to keep others from knowing it, though, God knows, it isn't often I go! I'm most ashamed of abstaining from meat when the Church commands it, and I wouldn't bless myself before Protestants if I got all the silver in the Wicklow mines. Now that's all for fear of the Protestants laughing at you—isn't it, Simon Kerrigan? Well! just look at the Bishop. Isn't he a good Catholic—every way you take him? he's never afraid or ashamed to do what the Church ordains—they say he'll never even go to a party of any kind with them unless it's some public occasion that he can't get over—still, there's ne'er a man in Boston—ne'er a one of their own ministers, may'be that they think so much of, or would go farther for. Think of that now, Simon! and hold up your head like a man for the time to come! Sure if you had the *spirit* of a man or an Irishman you wouldn't be ashamed of the religion that St. Kevin and St. Patrick belonged to, not to speak of all the rest of the saints from St. Peter down—*they* used to bless themselves, and fast, ay faith! and their fasting was no joke, for they kept it up most of the time, and hardly allowed themselves enough to keep body and soul together. Keep all this in mind, Simon, my boy! and it's proud you'll be of imitating the likes of them, and professing the faith that made saints of *them* !"

Buoyed up by such thoughts as these I had a spasmodic fit of religion, and while it lasted I considered myself quite chivalrous in manifesting my faith on every possible and impossible occasion. While under the influence of this temporary fervor, I was rather proud than otherwise of being the only one in the house who pretended to mortify the ancient Adam, and I actually had my hand up to my forehead to make the sign of the Cross one morning as we sat down to breakfast. Unluckily I caught John Parkinson's eye at the moment, and it seemed to me that it had a twinkle of fun in it, which I rightly attributed to the over-valorous action I was about to perpetrate. It is needless to say that the attempt was abortive as far as the blessing went. Running the culprit hand through my hair as though that were the ultimate object with which it sought my brow, I drew up my collar with a peculiarly independent air, and looked very hard at the picture of a greyhound on the wall before me. All this did not save me from the lash of John Parkinson's good-natured raillery. For many a day after he used to quiz me unmercifully about the blessing, especially the sheepish look I wore on the occasion.

On the following Sunday evening I was walking with Parkinson and another young Protestant friend of mine, down by the wharves along the banks of the Charleston river, when who should we meet but Philippus O'Sullivan strolling leisurely along with hands crossed behind his back and head bowed down in abstracted musing.

"Smoke the old fellow?" said Parkinson; "he looks as though we might poke some fun out of him, don't he?"

"Hush, hush!" said I, "that's my old master."

"What, O'Sullivan?"

"Exactly!"

"Better and better, I often wished to see the old codger, for I've a sort of notion that he's a queer customer. Hail him, Kerrigan! for if you don't he'll pass without noticing you. Go it, Simon! I'm just in want of something to make me laugh."

Thus urged, I accosted Philippus, who was as much surprised to see me as though I had suddenly been brought thither from the interior of Africa. I formally introduced my companions, and the old man returned their mock salute with a very low bow together with a very sincere expression of the pleasure he felt in making their acquaintance. At our joint request he turned back with us.

"How has it come to pass, Simon," said Mr. O'Sullivan, "that I have not seen you this last fortnight? I fear your thirst for knowledge is beginning to slacken."

"Oh! not at all, master, it ain't that, I assure you."

"It *ain't*, eh?" interrupted the worthy pedagogue, laying marked emphasis on the word *ain't*, "well if it *ain't* that, as you say, what *are* it?—oh, Simon! that I should hear you speak such grammar—did you, or did you not, ever learn the first rule of syntax? Tell me that now!"

Parkinson winked at Sharp, as much as to say: "What did I tell you?" and both made signs for me to continue the conversation which began so auspiciously for their hopes of "fun."

"Oh! never mind syntax now," I replied, affecting to be annoyed, "there's a time for all things. When I'm in school say what you like to me, but when I'm not in school, I don't want to be drilled—I won't have it, Mr. O'Sullivan, I tell you once for all."

The master looked aghast. He evidently doubted his own ears. "Tell me one thing, Simon! did you hear what the Bishop said last Sunday at High Mass about the reverence due to age?"

"I warn't at High Mass last Sunday," I returned snappishly, for I really began to feel somewhat nettled. "I never *go* to High Mass—it takes up too much of the one day we business-people have in the week—the only day we can call our own."

"Well, Simon," said the old man with a heavy sigh, "the Bishop said—"

"I don't care a cent *what* he said," snapped I again, determined to make a show of independence, especially as I saw my two companions smiling significantly at each other.

"A good evening, Mr. Kerrigan," said Philippus, cutting me very short and speaking very drily, "after that there's no use talking to you. It's only giving scandal we'd be to these worthy young men, and perhaps affording them a trifle of amusement into the bargain. It would be a great pleasure to me entirely to entertain them in any other way to the best of my poor abilities, and they'd be welcome to laugh at myself as long as they pleased, but in regard to religion it's a different thing altogether. The man or woman doesn't step in shoe leather that I'd allow to laugh at it or make little of it in my presence without raising my humble voice against it. I wish you all a very good evening!" And with the same old-fashioned, rustic bow as before, my old master turned and walked slowly away with a. air of offended dignity that made *me* laugh, although I felt exceedingly small, too.

Neither Parkinson nor Sharp joined in the laugh which surprised me not a little. I made no remark, however, and we walked on a few yards in silence. Parkinson was the first to speak:

"I say, Kerrigan, I think you got the worst of it that time, didn't you? Queer and all as he is, I rather think the old man had you there—eh, Simon?"

"Not he," I returned, in direct contradiction to the voice of conscience which inwardly pronounced a decided affirmative, "he's nothing better than a meddlesome old fool. I'll be done with him from this out."

I was not to be done with him quite so soon as I expected. It might have been some six weeks after, when I was sitting alone on one of the rustic seats on the Common, enjoying the rest which is always so sweet after a day of toil. The sunset was gilding the fine old trees which give grace and beauty to the undulating surface of the Common, and refreshing shade to the morning and evening walks of the good old people of Boston. One of these umbrageous canopies provided by the considerate care of some by-gone City-Council; now spread its gracious shade

over my head, and I was dreamily lounging away
the hour in the most perfect enjoyment of the *dolce
far niente,* when a well-known voice spoke at my
side, and a heavy hand, an authoritative hand, was
laid on my shoulder. The voice was that of Dominie
O'Sullivan, and it is hardly necessary to say that his
was the hand, too. I was not displeased at the *ren-
contre,* for, truth to tell, I had been thinking of home,
and of days which I could not help admitting were,
after all, the happiest I had yet known. I was thinking of my good, pious, simple old mother, of the
brothers and sisters from whom I knew myself de-
tached more than I chose to acknowledge even to my
own heart. With the family group came back to
my memory the long-revered image of Father
O'Byrne, whose simple, yet touching exhortations
resounded through my heart in the silence of that
evening hour. Though last, not least, in popped the
somewhat grotesque physiognomy of Patricius O'Grady, his lank form cased in frieze and corduroy, and
the ferule in his hand looking particularly threatening, yet I thought of the pedagogue then with unwonted kindness, and the "rule" which used to
make me "wither away for fear," was now nothing
more than a characteristic "accessory" to the portrait. It was just then that Philippus accosted me

as before mentioned, and I was rather pleased than otherwise at the interruption. Assuredly there was scarce another individual in Boston so closely afflil- iated to the scenes and persons that occupied my mind.

"I got a letter from your mother, Simon," said the old man after a few words of mutual inquiry had passed between us.

"You! you got a letter from my mother!" I ex- claimed in surprise; "why, what does my mother know about *you*, or you about her. It's very strange that she'd be writing to *you!*"

I looked hard at the Dominie, and, through the assumed look of innocence which sat awkwardly enough on his honest old face, I detected a certain confusion which betrayed the secret of the letter. My mind instantly misgave me that he had been doing what I then considered mischief, although now I see the action in a far different light. I was angry, yet I strove to conceal my vexation, and asked very quietly if I might see the letter.

No, he hadn't it about him, he said, he forgot it at the house beyond. Indeed, he hadn't the least idea that he'd meet *me*, when he went out for his even- ing walk on the Common. If he had, he'd surely have brought the letter.

7*

" What is it about ?" I asked rather sharply, being now confirmed in my suspicion.

" Well, most of it's about you—of course—dear knows I don't know what put it into your worthy mother's head to write to *me* of all people." He knew well enough, if he only chose to say so. I said it for him, however, and he neither denied nor admitted it, but went on as if he had not noticed what I said.

" It seems your mother—an excellent woman she is, too—has got it into her head that you're not as attentive to your religious duties as you ought to be. She says you're beginning to neglect *her*, and that that's a sure sign that you're neglecting your God."

" Me neglect her ! why, the old woman's raving, I guess. Didn't I send her twenty dollars about a month ago, and that's the last of sixty dollars I sent her altogether. Neglecting her, indeed ! I'd like to know what she expects from me !"

" I'll tell you that, my good Simon ; she expects the same love and affection from you as when you were at home, and without that, she says, she doesn't value all the money you'd send her. She's poor enough, she says, but still not so poor but she can do without your money, if your heart isn't what it used o be towards her, and she's a'most sure it is not from the way you write to her. She's in great trouble, too, about your soul, for fear it's losing your faith you might be, or living in a state of sin."

These words cut me to the quick, for I felt that they were only what I deserved. I bitterly reproached myself for my ingratitude which now stared me in the face, and had I been alone I would have shed many a repentant tear for the pangs I well knew I had caused my widowed mother. But O'Sullivan was beside me, his shrewd, deep-set eye fixed full upon me as though it would read my thoughts. This scrutiny I considered as a downright insult, and starting angrily to my feet, I said in tones of suppressed rage:

"I'd thank you, Mr. O'Sullivan, to mind your own business for the time to come, and leave me to mind mine. I'm very little obliged to you for writing to my mother about my affairs, and I'm just as little obliged to her for making so free with my name to a stranger."

"A stranger, Simon!" repeated the old man in a sorrowful tone; "am I a stranger to you, then?"

"Yes, you are, and worse than *any* stranger. I'll never speak a word to you again as long as I'm alive, unless my mind changes, and as for the foolish old woman that wrote such a blathering letter to you,

I'll touch her up for that same—never fear but I
will! When she gets any more money from me,
she may make medals of every dollar and give them
round the country for charms. Tell her that *you* in
your next epistle. Tell her, too, that I'm answerable
to God for my own actions and not to her, so she
needn't bother her head about me. I know my duty
better than she does—at least I hope so!"

"God help you for a poor foolish boy!" said Philippus solemnly, "and I'm afraid it's worse than foolish you are if the truth was known. If there's mercy
for you, take my word it'll be your mother's prayers
you may thank for it." So saying he stalked away,
and was soon lost in the dim perspective of the shady
avenue, leaving me to digest his words at leisure.

CHAPTER V.

MEANWHILE fortune continued to smile on me. Although slippery enough in regard to religion, I was both steady and assiduous in the discharge of my duty to my employers. The consequence was that I enjoyed their fullest confidence, and had my wages raised considerably at the expiration of the first year. Far different were the fortunes of poor Patt Byrne. A short time after my rupture with O'Sullivan I received a message from Patt requesting me to go to see, as he had got a hurt some weeks before that confined him to his bed ever since.

I started on hearing this, and a burning blush suf

fused my cheek. I had for the last six months entirely lost sight of the Byrnes, whom I looked upon
as no desirable acquaintances, inasmuch as they were
too old-fashioned in their tastes and habits for my
greatly-refined ideas. Patt was a laborer, too, and
so was his son Tommy, and as I had got at least two
steps higher than that, it was wholly impossible, in
fact a thing not to be expected, that I should continue
on the same terms with them. This conclusion was
forced on me by what I considered a very untoward
circumstance. I was one day going along Summer
street, on some business for my employers, dressed
in a very stylish "business-suit" of fine gray summer
cloth, and thought I was looking remarkably well,
whereat I was mightily pleased, for who should I meet
on turning a corner but the charming Miss Pringle,
a very stylish young lady, whose acquaintance I had
made at a public ball. Now Miss Pringle had the
honor of being forewoman to a French milliner in
Washington street, and it was commonly believed
that her old father, who had lived and died somewhere "away down East," had left her some hun
dreds of dollars. This, of course, gave additiona
attractions to a face and figure that were sufficiently
attractive of themselves. I was particularly pleased,
then, to meet Miss Pringle just when I was conscious

of being well dressed, and, indeed, Miss Pringle seemed just as glad to meet me, I suppose for the same reason, for she, too, was sporting her first crapes, and had the consoling testimony of her mirror at home that she looked not only lovely, but divine, in her exceedingly deep mourning. In my delight at seeing so welcome a sight that fine summer morning I had paid little attention to the fact that some men were working in a trench close by the sidewalk, where certain repairs were being made on the water-pipes. Who, then, can conceive my mortification and embarrassment, when, just as the young lady and myself had exchanged what we both thought a very polite salutation, a rough voice from the neighboring trench called out my name, with a " Bad-manners to you, Simy! is that you?"

I hardly knew which end of me was uppermost, so great was my confusion. The voice was that of Patt Byrne, and I must confess I could freely have performed that operation on his tongue which is said to give magpies the power of speech.

Without answering Patt's impudent inquiry as to my identity, I stole a look at Miss Pringle, who, in her turn, cast a penetrating glance at me.

"Good gracious, Mr. Kerrigan! are *you* Irish?" she asked, in a low voice, not so low, however, but Patt Byrne heard her.

"Is he Irish?" said he, popping his head up from the excavation. "'Deed, it's himself that is, and a dacent father and mother's child he is, too. It's myself that knows that well, for I seen him when he was little worth. When did you hear from the old woman, Simy?"

Muttering some indistinct reply, I nodded to Miss Pringle and walked on, annoyed by the contemptuous smile on her pretty face.

"Who'd have thought it!" she softly whispered, as I passed her by.

"Why, then, what in the world's got into that boy?" said Patt Byrne to his companion in the work of excavation, as he dived again under ground. Neither observation was lost on me, and I felt humbled, and could hardly tell why. The truth was, I had lost the good opinion of the fair Miss Pringle, who, I well knew, could never get over my being on such intimate terms with an Irish laborer, who certainly looked anything but "respectable" in his clay-soiled working clothes; as for Patt, I was probably done with his friendship, too, but of course that was of infinitely less importance.

I made several attempts to regain my place in Miss Pringle's favor, but all in vain, she ever after treated me with cool contempt as a person whom she did not or could not, recognize. The idea of ever again associating on equal terms with Patt Byrne and his family was too absurd to be entertained for a moment, and hence it was that I had cut the connection *in toto.*

Still, when I heard of Patt's misfortune, I reproached myself for having so long kept aloof from him and his, especially when I thought of the happy escape I had had from pretty Fan Pringle, who, a short time after my unlucky meeting with her on the street, had given her fair hand to a certain young master-tailor, who, on his part, got wofully bitten, for instead of receiving four or five hundred dollars with his "bonny bride," he had to pay a round hundred which she owed to the French milliner before mentioned.

It was with a feeling bordering on shame that I ascended the stairs to Patt Byrne's rooms, and my heart sank within me when I saw the condition to which the family were reduced in so short a time. Patt was sitting on a low chair with his right leg bandaged up and stretched on a stool before him. His face was ghastly pale and his eyes sunk far into their sockets. So great indeed was the change in his appearance that anywhere else I might have passed him by without knowing him. His wife, too, had lost the freshness of color which was hers by nature, and the Irish rose bloomed no longer on the chubby faces of the children. In short, they all seemed drooping and woe-begone, even the little rugged terrier, that had been so brisk and watchful, now hung his head as it were in hopeless melancholy, nor noticed my entrance except by a listless stare. I glanced my eyes around as I crossed the threshold, the family were all there except Tommy, whom I naturally concluded was at his work, and I mentally exclaimed " it's well they have him to earn for them."

My entrance was the signal for a burst of weeping from Nancy Byrne, and Patt himself, as he reached his hand to me, could hardly keep in his tears. I endeavored to console them as well as I could, and then asked how all this happened without my hearing a word of it.

" Ay! you may well ask that, Simy!" said Patt Byrne reproachfully; " we might be *all* dead it seems without your knowin' or carin'. God knows, then, if a less thing ailed you, it's in sore trouble we'd be about you, all of us."

I felt the truth of this, and, for a moment, could frame no answer. At last I ventured on some words of consolation. I had ascertained that Patt had broken his leg by a fall, and I muttered something about the trials that some people had to undergo in this world. "But after all," said I, "sure there's nothing bad but it might be worse. Things are bad enough with you now, it's true, but how would it be if you hadn't Tommy earning for you—then you might cry in earnest!"

This brought a torrent of tears from Nancy, and even Patt's eyes ran over, as he fixed them on me. "Ah, then, Simon Kerrigan!" said he in a voice that was hardly audible, "is that all you know about it?"

"About what?" I asked, with a sinking heart.

"Why, about our heavy sorrow—an' och! och! but that's what it is!"

"If it's the broken leg you mean, I know all about that, sure you told me yourself since I came in!"

"Oh *worra!*" said poor Patt, "if it was only that, I wouldn't regard it a pinch of snuff, God sees I wouldn't."

"Well, and what is it?" I asked, impatiently.

"We lost poor Tommy, Simy,—" Patt's voice failed him, and he covered his face with his hands, while a chorus of wailing arose from the mother and children. The blow unmanned myself, for I was altogether unprepared for such dismal tidings, and besides I really felt heart-sorry for the poor lad, who

was a fine, athletic, promising young fellow, with all
his father's good nature, and with no small share of
drollery in his composition. I knew not what to
say, even after I recovered the use of my speech,
and I can hardly tell what I did or what I said. I
did not dare to ask questions, every one of which
would have been a stab for each heart-wrung parent,
and I felt that consolation was beyond my power to
give. As well as I can remember I took Patt's hand
in silence and squeezed it very hard, and then going
over to Nancy I did the same to her, while the tears
that streamed down my cheeks evinced the sincerity
of my sympathy.

After a little, when grief had exhausted itself in
tears, the husband and wife dried their eyes, and
appeared comparatively calm.

" God bless you, Simy !" said Patt with touching
fervor, " may you never have to bear such a load of
sorrow as that poor woman and myself have on our
hearts this day. Yis, Simy, we have lost the best
son ever poor people had, a boy that wouldn't take a
shillin' out of his week's wages 'till he'd bring it
home an' put it in his mother's hand, an' if she'd
give him back a quarter or so, he'd be as thankful,
my poor boy ! as if it wasn't his own hard earnin'."

" True for you, Patt dear, true for you—oh ! Lord

look on us this sorrowful day!" This touching exclamation from the bereaved mother went to my
very heart—it spoke such a world of unutterable
woe.

It was some time before I discovered how poor
Tommy met his death. He had taken a heavy cold
which settled on his lungs, and finally turned to
inflammation, which carried him off in a few days.
He had been taken to the hospital for medical assistance, and there he died. About six weeks after, his
father fell from a ladder and broke his leg, and the
long illness which followed had exhausted the little
hoard so carefully preserved as the beginning of a
fortune.

"So here we are, you see," said poor Byrne, in
conclusion, with an attempt at cheerfulness that made
my heart ache; "here we are, Simy, as poor, ay!
and poorer than when we landed; we were layin'
out great things for ourselves, God help us! the very
last time you were here, but see how different things
have turned out; well, I suppose we must be content, whatever comes—only it was God's will it
wouldn't have come across us, that's all the comfort
we have, sure."

"But how in the world do you make out to live,
Patt?"

8*

" Well! myself could hardly tell you that—there'
none of these childer able to do much for us yet,
though they're willin' enough, poor things! if hey
had the ability—"

" You're forgettin' *me*, father!" said the second
son, Johnny, a lad of some fourteen years or so, and
he stretched up his little thick-set form to its highest;
" don't you know I'm able to work if I can only get
something to do."

" Dear help you, poor fellow!" ejaculated the fond
mother, " it's little you can do, I'm afeard."

" I'll soon let you *see* what I can do," said Johnny,
with quite a mortified air, " if Simon will only try
and get me in somewhere or other."

" That's just what I wanted to see you for, Simon,"
said Patt, as he stooped to move the disabled member
with both hands; " I know there's a good many
people employed where you are, and we were thinkin', Nancy and myself, that maybe you'd try to get
him in. If there's no place there for him, maybe
you'd know somebody that would give him work for
God's sake."

I smiled sadly at this. " If they don't employ
him for the sake of his broad little shoulders, Patt,
they'll hardly do it for God's sake. I'm afraid there's
no vacancy for the like of him about our place, but

I'll see what can be done. I'll come back soon, at any rate, with something better than words."

Blessings were heaped on me to no end, and I was hurrying away with a view to cut them short, when on the narrow and somewhat rickety stairs I encountered a person who, notwithstanding the bundle under his arm, I had no difficulty in recognizing as the great and good Bishop of Boston. I stepped back to the landing to let him pass, and he acknowledged the act by a salute as courteous as if I had been an emperor. I saw he was perfectly familiar with the place, and knew well where he was going, for he went straight to Patt Byrne's door, although several other dwellings opened on the same passage. The contents of the clumsy parcel which he carried were not known to me till my next visit to the Byrnes, but I felt that his errand was one of mercy, for Bishop Cheverus was the good Samaritan who, ubiquitous in his exhaustless charity, was found pouring oil on every wound, and ministering in whatever way he could to the wants and woes of his people.*

I afterwards found that his bundle contained

* It is related in the life of this most worthy prelate that he was very often seen carrying wood up several flights of stairs, to poor, destitute persons, and performing for the sick and infirm the most menial offices.

clothes which he had begged for Johnny, in order to
fit him out for a situation.   I had heard a great deal,
even from Protestants, of the good Bishop's charity,
but somehow the more I heard it talked of the less I
thought about it.   The thing had become as natural
as life, and it seemed a matter of course for every
one to talk about the acts of Bishop Cheverus.
Now that I saw him with my own eyes in the exer-
cise of his benign mission, my heart swelled within
me; I felt that such a man was, indeed, "little less
than the angels," and as far exalted above the aver-
age run of mankind as heaven is above the earth.

The sight of such God-like self-devotion brought me
back to a sense of what the world owes to religion,
and went far to revive the half-forgotten fervor of
my early years.   "Well, after all," reasoned I with
myself, "it would be a poor world *without* religion.
They may make fun of pious people as much as they
please, but when sickness or poverty comes across,
it's them that are always ready to lend a hand.   Some
will have it that religion is only a sham—maybe it is
with some, but not with all, I'll go bail.   Here's the
Bishop now—doesn't he do the same thing every
day of his life that we read of the Saints doing in
old times.   And, signs on him! there's not man, woman, or child in Boston that doesn't love the ground

he walks on. Well, it's a folly to talk, now, I must stir up, this sort of a dead-and-alive way that I'm in will never do. Please God, I'll go to my duty on Saturday next, and I'll write to my mother on Sunday, and I'll go to see poor O'Sullivan. I wonder how he's getting on!"

This frame of mind continued all that week, and I actually performed all I had promised. I bought a barrel of flour for Patt Byrne, and having heard of a situation that I thought might suit Johnny, I went to let them know; but found that the Bishop had been beforehand with me. He had himself got employment for the lad, to commence on the following Monday. This was a drop of joy in the cup of grief, but it hardly served to sweeten it. Dark, and dull, and heavy was the load of sorrow that weighed down the hearts of Patt Byrne and Nancy; and, as they afterwards told me, there were times when they were tempted to curse the day that saw them leave their native land, where they might still have had their son. But these thoughts were speedily repressed, the one rebuking the other for giving utterance to them : " Sure, didn't they know well enough, both of them, that their poor boy's hour was come, and he'd die all the same if he had been at home in the corner with his granny in Derrylavery. I'll war-

rant," said Nancy; "they heard the banshee this
time past about the ould place, for there's never one
belongin' to the Shanaghans that dies but she cries
them for weeks before. Och! och! it's little notion
they'd have that it was our Tommy beyant in America
she was cryin'."

Patt's leg, however, was rapidly improving, and
that was about the greatest consolation they could
all have, under the circumstances. In a couple of
weeks he was able to go back to his work; Nancy
and the children all watching his first departure from
the door with as much pride and satisfaction as if he
" walked in silk attire," and " siller had to spare,"
neither of which was poor Patt's case.

On the Sunday I wrote to my mother, and I think
she never got a letter from me so consoling to her
heart, for I felt as though it was but the day before
I had left her, and " the kind old friendly feelings "
came gushing out from my heart of hearts. I told
my mother how very careless I had been about religion—I told her very frankly; but assured her that
for the time to come I was going to turn over a new
leaf. I forgot to say, or even to think, " with God's
assistance," and so, like boastful Peter, I fell, but
unlike him, my fall was a fatal one.

Having finished my letter on that auspicious Sun-

day afternoon, I went to pay my intended visit to
Philippus O'Sullivan. The old man's reception of
me was kind as heart could wish; but I saw with
pain that he could not speak to me freely and openly
as of old. He tried hard to *appear* the same, but the
effort was too visible, and only made both of us un-
comfortable. There was little of the sarcastic in the
old man's composition, and yet he gave me more
than one severe cut during the hour that I staid with
him. I had been telling him of what the Bishop had
done for the Byrnes, winding up with a very sincere
expression of admiration for his saintly virtues.

" Yes," said Philippus, elevating his eyebrows, and
fetching a half sigh; " yes, he's a very worthy man,
they say—indeed, a God-fearing man, too—but, like
myself, he belongs to the old school—neither him nor
me has any great push in us as regards things mundane—"

I could not but feel that this was meant for me,
and I winced under the sting; but yet I could not
for my life help laughing when I looked at O'Sullivan
and heard im associate his own name and fame with
those of the eminent prelate, who might well be
called the Fenelon of America. I thought the old
fellow was serious, but not he indeed, for when I
burst out laughing, he laughed, too, in his own dry

unmusical way, then took out his box, gave it the professional tap, and handed it to me.

"Simon," said he, as I stood up to go, "I've a crow to pluck with you."

"So I thought, sir," I replied; "what is it? if it's about what happened down at the water-side that Sunday, you needn't say a word. There's no one sorrier for that than I am."

"It isn't that, Simon; I wish there was nothing worse than that. I'm told you're keeping company with a Protestant girl. I'd like to know if it's true."

"Well, it is not true—at the present time."

"Thank God for that, anyhow—all's well till that comes, Simon!"

"It'll never come, Mr. O'Sullivan!" I replied, in all sincerity.

"God grant it!" said Philippus earnestly, as he wrung my hand at parting. I went home in high spirits, rejoicing in the declaration I had just made, as if it were a point gained over the enemy of souls.

CHAPTER VI.

I WILL pass over the next four years of my life as being comparatively void of interest for the reader. During that time I had been gradually casting my shell, that is to say, the incrustation of superstition (as I learned to call the pastoral simplicity of my early life), which the teaching and example of credulous parents had formed on every faculty of my being; impeding the action of my natural intelligence, which I now discovered to be " of prime quality." This was the light in which I viewed the hideous skepticism that was fast taking root in my mind, growing up in rank luxuriance amongst the virtues that were spontaneous there. This baneful exotic threw its dark shade over the

9

fairest and brightest regions of my soul. I had long ago left off the practice of confession as something altogether too absurd for a young man of my pretensions. I still went to Mass occasionally—not, however, to High Mass, for I had no notion of being bored with tiresome sermons, and the Sundays were all too short for amusement. I had cut off all connection with the Byrnes, and poor Philippus O'Sullivan had been gathered—not to his fathers—but to the bosom of his mother earth. When he " shuffled off this mortal coil," it was a great relief to me, for he had dogged my steps in a way that fretted and annoyed me. He had even set the Bishop on me one time when I had grown more than usually careless about religion; and although I yielded to the good prelate's affectionate remonstrances, and for fully a year attended High Mass regularly, still I had a grudge at O'Sullivan for meddling in my spiritual affairs. I might never have discovered his transgression but for his own childish garrulity, and the secret did come out so artlessly, by way of a boast, that, with all my irritation, I could not help laughing heartily. That was but a year or so before the final summons came to poor Philippus, and when it did come, shame to say, I was not sorry. I never said a prayer more devoutly in my life than the " Rest

his soul!" which escaped my lips when I first heard
of his death. As I followed his funeral to the remote corner of the cemetery to which his poverty
consigned him, I was sensible of the same relief
which a man would feel after getting rid of a heavy
burthen which he had been forced to carry a long
and tedious way. My mother was too far away to
be much of a restraint on me—her advices and
admonitions, seen only by myself, and then committed
to the flames, were nothing more than a source of
amusement, and I could really afford to laugh at the
zeal which kept the old woman eternally fiddling,
like Paganini, on the one string. The case was far
different with O'Sullivan, who, as it were, at the door
with me, had his eyes ever on my motions, at least I
felt as though he had. The pertinacity with which
he interested himself in my affairs, do as I would, or
say as I would, was something altogether intolerable,
and the sense of his continual *surveillance* haunted me
like a spirit. The all-seeing eye of Providence had
lost somewhat of its terrors for me, and I could sin
with almost as much composure as though I had
never feared its scrutiny. Not so the eye of O'Sullivan, that living, speaking organ which told me, when
we met, as plain as any words could do, that I was
diverging from the way of life. It may well be sup-

posed, then, that the day of O'Sullivan's death was
then set down as a bright spot in my life. It was
so ; and I revelled in my sense of freedom like a bird
escaped from a cage.

Now that I can see men and things in their connection with the unseen world, my ancient master stands
before me in a different light, and his grotesque form
is enshrined within my heart as the casket that con
tained a Christian soul, sublime in its humble virtues,
many of which were known but " to the Father who
seeth in secret."

With the Philomath banished the last remaining
link that bound my aspiring soul to the lowliness of
earlier life.   As I stood by his lonely grave for a few
moments' thought, when all but me were gone, I said
within myself, " Now, Simon, you have just closed a
volume of your memoirs—you are free now to make
a start, and you can't but know that you have a glori-
ous opportunity.   Throw aside at once and for ever
the narrow bigotry which was all the inheritance left
you by your so-called ' pious ancestors '—they made
precious little of their piety as far as this world goes,
and, for that matter, I don't see that God ever willed
a whole people to remain for ages in the depths of
poverty—so I fear, Simon ! that the talk about being
' a chosen people ' and so on is all moonshine—the

fact is, those ' pious forefathers ' of yours were at all times behind the age, and had no more idea of getting along than—than that headstone there which expresses such a deal of filial devotion on the part of some excellent son. (Hope he didn't die himself of grief.) Keep the faith still, Simon, as, of course, you're bound to do, through thick and thin, but cast off as fast as ever you can the trammels of superstition; be a Catholic heart and soul, but a Catholic such as becomes this free and enlightened country. Courage now, Simon Kerrigan—ah-h-h!" what was it that caused that sudden twitch! my name, good reader, only my name. I had very soon found out after I came to Boston that the name which, with my religion, I inherited from my parents, was exceedingly vulgar, and had " such a common sound with it " that, as I used to say to myself, it proved beyond all doubt the plebeian origin which I would fain conceal from all the world. It makes me smile now to think of all the trouble that unlucky name gave me, especially when it smote my ear in an introduction. I always fancied that my acquaintances took a malicious pleasure in repeating the name oftener than was at all necessary, and on their foreign tongues it sounded so harshly, so uncouthly, that I thought there never was such a mean name. My cogitations at length ended, and the night at hand—a dark cheerless night, too—I made a precipitate retreat from a place which, of all others, had the least possible attractions for me.

It might have been some nine months after the death of my old master, that I one day overheard a conversation between Mr. Brown, the head of our firm, and a merchant from New Haven, who was one of our best *country* customers ever since I had been in the establishment, and, perhaps, long before it. This conversation, I could not, even at the moment, but apply to myself, and I soon found my surprise correct.

" I should be sorry to deprive you of him," said the New Haven gentleman, whose name was Samuels, " in case it put you to any *very* great inconvenience."

" Oh, not at all, I assure you," broke in Mr. Brown, eager to oblige so good a customer, " not at *all*—we have so many here—in fact, too many for our present requirements—but even if it *be* a trifling sacrifice on our part, it will give us the greatest pleasure, inasmuch as it affords us an opportunity of showing the interest we take in your affairs. Besides, we here in Boston can more easily provide a substitute, than you in New Haven. There is one thing

however, concerning this young man which I think
you ought to know."

I could see from where I was that Mr. Brown
looked grave, and Mr. Samuels elevated his spectacles
so as to peer inquiringly into his friend's face with
his own visual orbs.

" And what may that be ?" he inquired anxiously.
" No bad habit, eh ? nothing against his moral
character, I trust."

" Well! not exactly—but still you may think it
bad enough.   The young man is a Papist."

" A Papist ! you *don't* say so, Mr. Brown !"

" But I *do* say so, Mr. Samuels !"

" Well! you really surprise me—you do—how *did*
you come to employ him ?"

" We took him at the request of a friend in whose
employment he had been as porter, and I must say
we have never had any serious fault to find with him.
Neither will you, I am persuaded.   Even though he
is a Catholic he really does get along well.   The
offensive tenets of that religion—"

" Re-lig-ion, Mr. Brown! say, rather, supersti
tion !"

" Well! be it so—the offensive tenets of that
hideous superstition he keeps to himself admirably
well, I assure you—so that you would scarce know

he wore its fetters, if you didn't find it out some other way."

"Then you think I might venture to take him?" queried Samuels, slowly; "it would be, I know, considerable of a risk, for I never *had* anything to do with one of those people, an I hadn't got any faith in them. Still I rather like this young man—he has a real good method of doing business, and I do want a smart, active young man very bad—very bad, indeed! You say he keeps it all to himself—I mean the grosser features of the superstition."

"Certainly!"

"Um! aw! it is most unfortunate—just what I least expected—but still my need is pressing. I think I shall try him, Mr. Brown!"

"Very good, sir! just walk into the warehouse, where you will, I believe, find him. I will leave you to talk the matter over between yourselves. If it were any other but yourself, Mr. Samuels, it would go hard on us to part with him, but to you, as I have said, we are quite willing to transfer our rights over the property —ha! ha! ha!"

Mr. Samuels soon after came to me in the warehouse, and, after some preliminary chat, during which he was evidently "beating about the bush," he darted right into the subject, and made his proposal in due form. I affected to be much surprised, and expressed considerable reluctance to leave my present employ. ers. In this I was quite sincere, for I had been, on the whole, well treated by them, and had no reason therefore, to be dissatisfied. My objections were easily overruled, for Mr. Samuels, after some parley, offered me such a tempting salary that I couldn't longer think of refusing his offer, and I agreed to go to New Haven early in the following week, (my engagement was weekly at Brown & Steensons.)

I was surprised that the New Englander made no allusion to the obnoxious nature of my religious "opinions," but he was only leaving that point for the last. Just as he took up his broad-brimmed hat to retire, he fetched an asthmatic "hem!" and approach ing quite close to me, said in a hesitating sort of tone, "Mr. Brown tells me—what indeed I did not expect to hear—ahem!—that you are a—a—Catholic!"

"I am, sir—but what of that?"

"Oh nothing—nothing at all—I hope we shall get along together as though you warn't—but—but—it would ruin the business if I were known to have a partner of your persuasion. You have no *idea* how Papists are disliked down our way. You han't indeed! Can't you oblige me now by making no one the wiser as to what you are?"

" But, sir !" I said with a smile, " it will be useless for me keeping the secret so long as I am seen attend-ing the Catholic Church. The murder *will* out, you see."

" Oh! if it's only that, of course I ain't afraid, ecause, you see, we haven't got any Popish meeting-house within many a mile of us. You must pray at home, Mr. Kerrigan—ha! ha! only promise to say nothing about what you are, and we shall get on swimmingly. I won't mind if you *do* say Mass in your own room once in a while, or count over your beads, or anything of that kind. Oh, no! Mr. Ker-rigan, you will find me a very tolerant man—very tolerant, I assure you! no matter *how* mistaken oth-ers may be in their religious views, I can make all allowance—I can, indeed, Mr. Kerrigan !"

Though much amused at the good man's idea of " saying Mass," I thought any attempt at enlighten-ing him would be so much labor lost ; I, therefore, thanked him for his promised stretch of liberality, and prepared with a hopeful heart, and with the pleasurable excitement which young people always feel when about to " visit parts unknown," to enter upon my new situation.

I bade farewell to Boston with little regret. Few ties of friendship had I there to make my departure painful. John Parkinson had gone to New York to live some three years before, and I had quarrelled with O'Hanlon soon after his marriage, on account of a biting sarcasm levelled at my religious indifference one evening by his wife, who was a fervent Catholic, much more fervent indeed than Harry. I thought O'Hanlon ought to have taken sides with me, whereas he did not; but, on the contrary, seemed to enjoy my confusion. I was too proud to appear to take any notice of the affair at the time, but I never could endure Mrs. O'Hanlon after, and my warm friendship for Harry became suddenly icy cold. It was the last evening I ever spent at their lodgings, where I had spent many a pleasant one before. With the O'Hanlons went my last chance of Catholic society. Never again did I form an intimate connection with any Catholic, male or female, for even if I were inclined to do so, I had no opportunity in the new and strange position to which Providence—shall I say Providence?—assigned me.

For some weeks after my arrival in New Haven all was strange, and dull, and cheerless to me. Even now, after the lapse of some five-and-thirty or forty years,* the State of Connecticut is, perhaps, the most Puritanical in the Union, and consequently the most op-

* We are to suppose that this was somewhere about 1850.

posed to the general and enlivening spirit of Catholicity. What must it have been, then, at the time
when I took up my abode in the family of Deacon
Samuels, for such was the spiritual office of my new
employer. A ruler in Israel, an ancient of the people
was he, grave and melancholic in temperament, yet
upright and honest in his dealings, and withal rather
kind-hearted. He was a worthy man in his own
peculiar fashion, and had naturally very little of that
bile in his composition which, in regard to Papists,
he was obliged to manifest exteriorly, as, without it,
he could not maintain that influence which his high
pretensions to godliness gave him in the community.

The family of Deacon Samuels consisted at this time
of a maiden-sister whose grand climacteric was at least,
ten years back in the past, and a son of sixteen, named
Josiah, a tall and rather clumsy youth whose precocious gravity gave great hopes of future distinction
amongst the elect. I was told that Josiah had a
sister who was away somewhere seaward on a visit,
but as none of the family spoke of her, I, of course
made no inquiries concerning her. From the tone
in which my informant mentioned the young lady, I
knew not what to think of her, other than this, that
she was esteemed no credit to the house of Samuels.
The surmise to which this impression gave rise in my

mind was strengthened if not confirmed by the dead silence which reigned in the house concerning her. " She must be no great things," said I to myself. " when they seem to feel her absence so little."

The demerits of Miss Samuels, the younger, if demerits she had, were amply made up for to the community in general by the rare qualities of her Aunt Olive, who, good lady ! was looked up to still more on account of her evangelical virtues than her commanding stature, which, together with her high-heeled shoes, elevated her far above all female competitors.

Such was the family into which I was happily and most graciously introduced by the worthy patriarch who was its ostensible head. *Ostensible*, I say, for I afterwards found out that Miss Olive, not he, wielded the domestic sceptre.

CHAPTER VII.

BOUT a month after I had taken up my abode in the house of Deacon Samuels, (where to say the truth I was as well treated as heart could wish,) I was one morning disturbed out of a pleasant dream by the sound of voices clattering and talking at a prodigious rate in the garden without, and almost under my window. Starting up in a fright supposing I had overslept myself, I first to ran my watch and found it only a few minutes past six, which was my usual hour for " turning out." Finding all right in that direction I next hastened to the window, and lifted the smallest possible bit of the snowy blind, with a view to discover what the noise meant at that early hour of the morning. The speakers were not to be seen from where I was, they being close to the wall underneath, but I speedily re-

nised one of the voices as that of Miss Olive.
The other was a female voice, too, but it sounded
strange to me, although somehow I liked its tones,
for they were clear and silvery, ay! and mirthful,
too, like the warbling of a linnet or a thrush.

" It ain't any use to talk so, aunt!" said the musi-
cal voice, and its tones waxed somewhat sharper and
higher, " I don't care if he do hear me—I say you
had no *business* to give him my room, and I will have
it this very day. An attic-room is quite good enough
for father's clerk, and so you should have known—
all of you!"

The aunt tried to soothe the ruffled young terma-
gant, as I inwardly styled her, but her efforts were
thrown away, at least while the pair were in my
hearing, and as they walked away together, still invisible to me, the debate proceeded fast and warm.

"So," said I to myself, as I made my hurried toilet,
" this is a fine specimen of a godly young puritan. I
suppose she arrived some time in the night. And
she wants to eject my poor self in a summary manner, I see. Well! I'm sorry to leave this pretty
room, for I don't think there's another like it in the
house—but, of course, her ladyship must have her
way and her room into the bargain. ' I will have it
this very day!' To be sure, Miss Brimstone! it isn't

me that would keep you out of it—much good may
it do you, when you get it !—' it ain't any use talk
ing so, aunt !'—oh ! of course not, you young spawn
of the covenant ! you have it in you. I'll go bai
you're bitter as soot, and as sharp as a razor ! Well!
I don't wonder now at their being so careless about
her. I'll be bound she keeps the house in hot water
for them when she's in it !"

Feeling anything but comfortable in the conscious
ness of having the spoiled daughter of the house
prejudiced against me beforehand, I looked forward
with no very pleasant sensations to the prospect of
meeting her at breakfast, and when eight o'clock came,
I left the store with a heavy heart, and entered the
parlor with, I must confess, a very sheepish air. At
the first glance, I thought I had the room to myself,
and I felt ever so much relieved. I was mistaken,
however, for I had hardly taken a seat—which I did
near one of the front windows—when a light rustling
sound at the farther end made me start and look
around. O ye fates ! half buried in an old arm-chair
near the back window right opposite where I sat,
was the daintiest little sylph that ever floated on a
moonbeam, and looking at me from behind some stray
curls, with the drollest expression imaginable, were
a pair of eyes that seemed formed for mischief—a

malicious pair of orbs they were, if my judgment went for anything—and as I caught their expression of supercilious mockery, evidently directed to myself, I winced as though an adder had stung me. Still the face to which these eyes belonged was so very— shall I say beautiful—no, *piquant* rather, and bright and sparkling, that it riveted your gaze in spite of you. I was at the same time attracted and repelled, and although I took up a book which fortunately lay in my way, and pretended to be much engrossed by its contents, still I could not for my life help stealing a glance now and then at the bright apparition in the arm-chair. She, it appeared, was amusing herself at the expense of my evident perturbation, for almost every time that I looked towards her I was so unlucky as to meet her eye, and then she was sure to look still more arch, as if to increase my embarrassment. At last she fairly laughed out, and for my soul I could not help laughing, too, whereupon the young lady arose and came some yards nearer to where I sat, as if to show off her exquisite little figure, then threw herself coquettishly on a sofa and laughed again with that girlish air at once so artless and so full of fun. At length she spoke:

"I shouldn't wonder, now, if you were father's new—the young gentleman from Boston!"

"I shouldn't wonder if I were," said I, involun
tarily catching her sportive manner.

"Mr. Ker—Ker—what's the rest of it?"

A bright thought flashed on me, suggested by Miss
Samuels' attempt at pronouncing my name. "There
ain't any more of it," said I, "my name is Kerr—
Simon Kerr, at your service."

"Kerr!—why that *is* funny, now—I thought aunt
said your name was Ker-gan, or something that
sounded horrid Irish—are you sure your name is only
Kerr?"

"Quite sure, miss!—people *have* sometimes put an
addition to it in the way you mention—but that was
only amongst the lads in our office, who did it for a
lark—my name is Kerr, I assure you!"

The rest of the family now came in, and as breakfast was already on the table, we took our seats at
once, after a formal introduction of me to Miss Samuels, and of Miss Samuels to me by her father as
"my daughter Eve—Mr. Kerrigan!" The introduction I felt to be superfluous, and so did Miss Eve,
too, as she contrived to make me understand by
furtive look of sly meaning. The introduction over,
I took occasion to set the seniors and Josiah right as
regarded my name, whereat the Deacon expressed
his satisfaction inasmuch as my *real* name had much

the advantage of the nickname in point of respectability. The good man was quite indignant at the
liberty which the good-for-nothing young Boston-
ians had taken with my patronymic. It is needless
to say that ever after I was known to the Samuels
and all New Haven as *Mr. Kerr*. Bless the mark!
many a time I laughed in my sleeve as I thought how
nicely I had gulled the Irish-hating New Englanders,
but the laugh was turned the other way, as I fancied
how my mother and the "folks at home" would feel
if *they* heard me addressed by a name so unfamiliar
to Irish tongues or Irish ears. The Deacon looked
at me with no small surprise when he first heard his
daughter address me by my new cognomen, and per-
ceived that I answered it as naturally as possible.
The wicked device of my Boston comrades which
had given such an awkward addition to my name was
then explained, much to the good man's gratification,
for "somehow he never could take to that there
name of Kerrigan, or get his tongue right about it—
and besides, it always made folks stare to hear it in
his store, it sounded so Irish-like!"

This point happily settled, we "men-folk" swallowed our breakfast with due dispatch, and proceeded
to the dispatch of business in the store at the corner
of the next block. When night came I was shown

to a bed-room very different indeed from that which had previously occupied, not, however, without an elaborate apology from the elder Miss Samuels.

"I hope you won't find it hard of me, Mr. Kerr!" said the formal spinster, "it ain't my fault, I assure you. It's all along of that self-willed Eve, who insisted on having her room back again, and no other room would she have. She's an awful girl that, Mr. Kerr! Her heart is as dry—as dry as powder—the dew of heavenly grace has never watered it, nor never will, I guess, for the child is so proud, so obdurate, I might say, that I have no hopes of her—none in the world!—oh! what a house we should have without her. I would that some charitable Christian man would take her to himself, for her own father is ashamed of her unregenerate spirit!"

"A charitable wish," thought I, "for the Christian man—her own father cannot manage her, and yet you would have another undertake the job. A precious piece of goods she must be, this Miss Eve. And yet"—what I further soliloquized after closing my room-door, any young gentleman of twenty-two may imagine who has ever been "struck" as I was by the sudden apparition, when least expected, of a bright-eyed, roguish lovely girl of eighteen, breaking in on the dullest and most monotonous of lives.

Suffice it to say, that I was quite willing to excuse her faults, patent as they were to every beholder.

"How do you feel in your new chamber, Mr. —— what's your name?" said Miss Eve to me with provoking indifference when we met next morning very, very early, at a sharp angle of one of the garden walks. I don't know what took us both out so early that morning.

"Much exalted," I replied, "and entirely obliged to *you* for my sudden promotion, which is altogether beyond my merits."

"Oh, you are too modest by half, Mr. Kerr!" She remembered my name this time. "Many of your countrymen attain much higher promotion than that in this Western World—though I'm sorry to say they thank people as little for ' drawing them up ' as you do me for sending you to the upper story." It needed not the significant motion by which the saucy girl pointed to her delicate neck to show that she meant anything but a compliment, and otherwise her words were not very pleasing to me.

" *My* countrymen, Miss Samuels ?"

"That's just what I said!—I guess you think I don't know what you are. But you can't blindfold *me*, I tell you. There's that about you that's too Irish to be got rid of, though you try ever so hard

There! don't look so angry—it ain't any use to leny it. I see you want to, but *don't*—I han't got anything against the Irish, for all I do speak hard of them once in a while. If you ain't a Papist, *I* don't mind your being Irish, though father and aunt and all the folks about here have a perfect horror of them—they have indeed!"

Where was the use of denial under these circumstances? and resentment, or the appearance of it, would have only given Eve an opportunity of laughing at my petulance, so I had nothing for it but to admit the fact, and compliment the young lady on her penetration.

"And now that you have my confession!" said I, "I have no doubt but you will take good care to make it public—especially as you seem quite conscious that it would injure me."

"I'll do just as I have a mind to, Mr. Kerr!—I always do: if I thought it would really spite you I might whisper it to a confidential friend who would soon set numerous other confidential tongues agoing on the subject, and it would be all up with your pretensions to respectability—but—it all depends on how you act."

I was just going to inquire, half jest and whole earnest, what line of conduct would be most likely to meet her approbation, when she smiled and nodded in the direction of the house, and looking that way I saw, to my utter dismay, the Deacon himself approaching,

"With reverend step and slow."

I was for making my escape under cover of the pyramidal box-wood near which we stood, but Miss Eve commanded me to keep my ground, and stooping she plucked a leaf of trefoil which grew at her feet, and handed it to me.

"Come quick, father," she said to the old man, who certainly looked rather sourish as he approached, and glanced from one to the other of us with an uneasy aspect; "*can* you tell us—for being a Deacon you ought to know more than others—whether this three-leaved plant is a descendant of the weed so loved of Irishmen, or if not—how came it here? Mr. Kerr here, though never having seen an Irish shamrock, will have it that this is a spurious article, not even a cousin of the other." Oh! the wicked glance that shot upward at me from under the long lashes!

Much relieved, apparently, by this ingenious though simple stratagem, the old man declared that he knew very little of such matters, not being overstocked with book-learning.

"And indeed I think *you'd* be better in your bed, Eve Samuels!" he curtly added, "than studying botany before sunrise. Go in, child, and help Rachel to prepare the breakfast."

Eve tripped away with the brightest of smiles, after pinching the grave old man on the cheek and laughing heartily at his " Shame, shame, Eve!—will you never learn to conduct yourself as a Christian maiden should ?"

I saw nothing un-Christian in the girl's conduct, yet I did not wonder at what her father said, for it must be confessed there was as little of the Puritan about her as though she had been nurtured in France or Ireland. I was roused from a reverie into which I was falling by the voice of Deacon Samuels.

" Mr. Kerr—" said he, and then he stopped, " Mr. Kerr! it ain't pleasant to have to speak of the faults of our own flesh and blood, but I do hope you'll not be scandalized at the thoughtless levity of this child's conduct."

" Scandalized, Mr. Samuels! why, I see no fault in her!" I spoke more warmly than I intended, and the old man looked up at me with a peculiar expression, as he replied

" You don't, eh?—you must be very lax in your notions of female propriety, then!"

" Well! I don't know that I am, sir!—however, that's neither here nor there—I had no intention of giving an opinion on your daughter's merits, which I would consider a great liberty on my part. Surely you would not have me speak hard of her in *your presence.*"

" Why no, Kerr!—come to think of it, you couldn't well do that. But I may speak of her myself as she deserves—with a view to prevent you from being scandalized by her fantastical ways. I hope you have noticed that she is altogether different from the rest of us."

" I have, indeed, Mr. Samuels!—the difference is quite perceptible."

" Very good, ve-ry good, *indeed.* And I guess you have been puzzled to know how she came to be as she is."

I thought it best to answer by an affirmative nod, as I knew not well what I could say with safety.

" Well, now, I know Olive would soon tell you all about it, so I may as well have the first of it. You must know that Eve's mother was a Frenchwoman."

" A Frenchwoman!" I repeated with unfeigned astonishment.

" Yes, a Frenchwoman!"

" And a Catholic?"

11

It was the Deacon's turn to look astonished, whxch he did, and somewhat nettled, too! he drew himself up and looked me full in the face with a counten ance quite evangelical, it was so bitter. "Now, Mr. Kerr! I want to know," said he very slowly, his words gathering intensity of emphasis as he pro- ceeded, " I *want* to know do you, or do you *not*, mean to insult me!"

I, of course, eagerly disclaimed any such intention.

"Well, then, sir, never—as long as you and I live under the same roof—never so far forget what is due to my character as to hint, or insinuate the possibility of my ever having consorted with a Papist. No, sir! it was my misfortune to fall in with a French- woman—a Protestant, of course—when I was a giddy lad serving my time to a dry-goods merchant in Bos- ton."

" I should like to have seen you when you were a ' giddy lad,' " I said within myself, but, of course, it *was* within myself.

"The young woman was comely," went on the Deacon, " a well-favored damsel and well spoken, too, and I met her often at the house of a relative of mine whose ways were according to the flesh. I was giddy, as I told you, and like a little fish that plays around the fatal bait till it can no longer resist its

.onging, and snatches greedily at its ruin, so I was attracted by this ' strange woman' (as the good book forcibly styles the unregenerate daughters of the enemies of God's people), till my heart was ensnared. I swallowed the bait, hook and all, and took the foreigner to my bosom, and since that hour remorse has settled on me like a blood-sucker, and the effects of my sin are still with me in the daughter that Angèle left behind her when she died. Woe is me ! she has the comeliness of her unhappy mother, and her hard, unregenerate spirit that mocks at the workings of divine grace."

" But was your wife's conduct really bad or objectionable ?" I inquired with much curiosity.

" No, no—according to this vain world she was a good wife and a good mother, for the short time she lived with me, but oh ! the lightness, the levity, the un-Christian levity of that woman was beyond description. She was worse than her daughter, I *do* think, and you may judge from that what manner of wife she made me."

I was strongly tempted to laugh in his face, but I knew that would make him my enemy for life, so I stretched *my* face to a sympathetic length, and cast about for something to offer by way of consolation. Fortunately I had it at hand, for I just caught a glimpse of Josiah, crossing the alley with that precocious heaviness of step and gravity of countenance which made him a juvenile pillar of the conventicle.

"It is happy for you, sir," said I, " that the late Mrs. Samuels left you one promising subject—Mr. Josiah seems to take after your side of the house."

"I thank my Maker he *is* a good lad," said the Deacon with a sudden change of manner; " he grows in wisdom and in grace."

" In *grease* certainly," said I to myself, as my eyes again fell on Josiah who was somewhat of the fattest for his years.

" But his superabundance of grace came not to him from Angèle Dupré—"

" No ?—who, then ?"

" Why, from his own mother, a godly woman, who was a shining light here in New Haven, where I took her to wife after it pleased Heaven to take Angèle hence. Mercy Heavyside was indeed a rare woman —a woman endowed with the Spirit's best gifts— would that she had lived longer, for she might have overcome the rebellious heart of my unhappy Eve—"

We were here summoned to breakfast. During the meal, I noticed Miss Eve glancing at me occasionally with an expression half humorous, half inquisitive which I was at no loss to understand, but I dared not give even one explanatory look, for I felt that three pair of lynx eyes were upon me.   As for Eve, she seemed to take a malicious pleasure in teasng her aunt and mimicking her grave brother, to the evident annoyance of her father, who was, nevertheless, forced to laugh at times in a very undeaconlike manner.

11*

CHAPTER VIII.

THE aspect of things was completely changed in the Deacon's household after the return of Eve. The still water of our daily life was now perpetually in motion, curled hourly and momentarily by some delightful little whim of Eve's, set down by her staid and sober relatives as a fearful back-sliding. Dullness was forthwith banished from the house, driven hence, it would seem, by the sparkling smile and mirthful voice of our Euphrosyne. To her father, aunt, and brother, the change was torture, but to me it was delightful—quite a relief. It is true there was little sympathy between myself and Eve. We were always carping at each other, and hardly ever agreed on any one

subject, yet this very disagreement had in it a kind
of strange charm.   In spite of myself I was attracted
to the wild, witty, provoking little damsel who seemed
bent, morning, noon, and night, on thwarting and
annoying me in every possible way.   The very sight
of her freshened up my wits and set them sparkling
and frothing like champagne.   I thought it was a
spirit of emulation that moved me to foil the girl
with her own weapons, and so I encouraged it, little
dreaming of its real character.   It did startle me a
little at times when I found myself so continually occupied with the thought of " what Miss Eve would
say to this," and " what Miss Eve would think of
that," but I easily managed to get over my uneasiness, for every time the pair of us entered into conversation she nettled me so in one way or the other
that for the time I was positively angry, and wondered
very innocently how any one *could* possibly like that
tormenting little minx.   Part of her system of annoyance was to keep me continually on the stretch
about my unfortunate country.   Twenty times a day
she was, or appeared to be, on the point of letting
out my secret, and my imploring look only made her
laugh.   Still she always managed to avoid making
any disclosure, adroitly changing the conversation
just when my fears were wound up to the highest

pitch, and perhaps, too, the curiosity of others pre
sent who would, doubtless, have enjoyed such an exquisite morsel of scandal as that of Mr. Kerr's being
convicted of Irish birth.   As regarded my religion I
had little or no apprehension, for the Deacon was the
only one who knew it, and his interest, together with
the credit of his establishment, alike bound him to
secrecy.   Even to myself he made no allusion to it,
and I sometimes thought that he forgot all about it,
as, for instance, when he so earnestly besought me
not to be scandalized at the delinquency of his daughter.   I was mistaken, however ; Mr. Samuels did *not*
forget that I was a Papist, but he wanted to make *me*
forget it, and in this he was excellently well assisted
by the peculiar circumstances in which I was placed.
The whole of New England was at that time one
vast mission under the pastoral care of the Bishop of
Boston.   The Catholics were comparatively few, and
scattered here and there in little knots and groups
throughout the New England States, without priest
or church, except when the charity of the Boston
clergy impelled them to visit the remote parts of the
immese diocese on a mission.   I was, therefore, com
pletely isolated, for although there were, doubtless,
many other Catholics in New Haven, I neither knew
them, nor they me.   My intercourse was exclusively

with Protestants of the evangelical school, and they
never appeared to suspect me even of Popish *proclivity*. They had a notion, I could see, that I was
rather lax in my views, but that was nothing more
than often occurred to good father and mother's children. Go no farther than Eve Samuels, who had
been nurtured in godliness, and fed on sound doctrine ever since — ever since her mother's death.
Mine was just a similar case, the old ladies of the
town seemed to think. By my name I must be
Scotch, for the Kerrs were most all lowland Scotch
folk, and, no doubt, I had had a pious, God-fearing
mother, not to speak of my paternal parent, but I
had been so long amongst " the tribe of the ungodly "
in Boston, that I had fallen into the slough of indifference. I believe my name and Eve's were often coupled in public prayers at the meeting-house which
the Deacon and his family attended. This was capital fun to Eve, and many a good laugh she had herself at the pious exercises practiced in her behalf.
But the laugh was all to herself, for as often as I was
moved to mirth by her serio-comic account of the
zeal with which our joint conversion was sought after
in the conventicle, she instantly stopped short and
rebuked me with well-feigned displeasure. It was
my greatest consolation that she knew nothing of

my real religious " opinions,' and I felt ever so grateful to her father for keeping the matter secret.   This cowardly concealment of my faith I easily accounted for to my conscience by the specious pretext that when there was neither church nor priest, nor any opportunity of practicing the duties of religion, there was no necessity for my making idle professions which could only subject me to ridicule and contempt. " Yes !" said conscience, " that is all very fine, Mr. Simon *Kerr !*—ahem ! but how will you account for eating meat on Fridays and Saturdays ?   You were terribly angry with poor O'Hanlon some years back for doing the same thing, what have you now to say for *yourself*, when you do it to make folks believe that you are what you are not ?—eh, Simon ?—what would the old woman at home say if she saw you gorging yourself three times a day with forbidden meats ?—what would Father O'Byrne say, either ?"

As I never was able to answer this with any degree of satisfaction, I generally snubbed " the inward voice " at this point, and manfully asserting my independence, said I didn't care a snap for either of them, I'd eat *what* I pleased, and *when* I pleased   Many other things I said to conscience in regard to its being meddlesome and intrusive, and I know not what, but somehow, bluster as I would, conscience never

oould be convinced nor yet silenced, and I was obliged
to admit, moreover, that it always had the best of
the argument. Logic and rhetoric were alike at
fault in discussing matters with conscience, which, in
fact, I found a very tyrant, for it would hear no ex
use, extenuate no fault, or connive at any weakness,
where duty was concerned. It was a thorough-going
inquisitor of a conscience, as I used to think, and its
punishments were quite as severe as any inflicted
(in romance) on the tender victims of inquisitorial
malice.

The hardest thing of all, however, was Eve's biting
allusions in regard to my not going to church. It
did not appear to me that she cared what church I
oelonged to, or whether I belonged to any, and still
she kept harping on the subject I supposed from pure
spite.

"Do you never go to church?" said she to me
with her usual abruptness, on the third Sunday after
her return.

"Not in New Haven," I laconically replied.

"And why so?"

"There ain't any church here where the preacher
comes up to my ideas of Christian doctrine."

"There ain't, eh? and what may *your* ideas be, Mr.
Kerr?"

" You wouldn't be anything the wiser if I were to tell you."

" You're very polite indeed, Mr. Paddy."

" I am about as polite as some of my neighbors, Miss Eve—I can't but be obliged to you for that nickname you gave me. There's your father calling you."

" I'm not deaf, I thank you. But do tell me," and her voice softened a very little, " do tell me what religion you profess."

" Another time, Miss Eve !—when I feel disposed for confession. Will that do ?"

" No, it won't do, and I'll tell you what, Mr. Kerr, you'd best not put me to guessing. I might possibly guess something that you wouldn't like."

I shrank, without knowing why, from the piercing glance that rested on my face, and I actually felt my cheek glow. I knew not what I had best say, and was still hesitating as to what I *would* say, when a low mocking laugh from our first mother's malicious namesake made me start and look towards her. She was about to leave the room, and had turned back with a warning gesture, accompanied by the strange, startling laugh I have mentioned.

" So you won't tell !"

" What can I tell ?—there's no preacher here whose

doctrines meet my approbation. That's all, I assure you."

"No, it ain't all—you know it ain't, but I'll get to the bottom of it some day, and then—look out for yourself!"

On another occasion she pressed me so close that I was fairly cornered, and I told her half jestingly, and by way of a pun, that I was a Universalist.

"Universalist!" she repeated very slowly, eyeing me at the same time with a very scrutinizing look. "That's an odd religion for an Irishman—how did you come by it?"

"That's a secret?"

"Not to me, for I don't believe you're anything of the kind."

"And why not, Miss Eve?"

"Why, because you Irish, unless you're greatly belied, are more prone to believe too much than too little—in fact you're too superstitious to be a Universalist or any such thing!"

Having no very clear idea of the extent to which Universalism was opposed to superstition, as insinuated by Miss Eve, I thought it best to beat a retreat, the ground on which I stood being so untenable; I, therefore, made a very low bow, and thanked the young lady on behalf of my countrymen.

I had been about half a year in New Haven when the entire town was thrown into commotion by the news that a Catholic priest from Boston had arrived for the purpose of holding a mission. At first the report was considered incredible, and the gossips were sharply rebuked by the more godly among the inhabitants for giving circulation to such scandalous rumors. In due time, however, the report was found to be but too true ; a very mysterious-looking individual suddenly made his appearance in the quiet streets, closely buttoned up in a tight-fitting black surtout, gliding here and there in the quietest and and most Jesuitical manner possible. Quite a Popish-looking character he was described to me, although those who had seen him felt bound to admit that he seemed to be " rayther a decent-looking man," which, under the circumstances, was quite remarkable.

All that day there was nothing talked of but the Popish priest, his dress, his appearance, with the probable object of his visit, for the meaning of the word *mission* was by no means clearly understood. Various speculations were afloat, and more than the usual amount of guessing was done on the occasion, but, of course, all was shrouded in mystery, and no one was any wiser than his neighbor, at least amongst the inhabitants proper.   Miss Olive was in a state of nervous excitement from morning till night,—and from night till morning, I suppose, too—for at the breakfast-table she appeared each morning with such an increase of haggardness and attra-biliousness on that leaf of flesh which is said to contain the index of the mind, that it was quite plain she had not wooed the drowsy deity, or, wooing, found him unpropitious; which Eve and myself set down to her anxious curiosity concerning the priest.   Poor man! how innocent he was, or appeared to be, as he walked our streets, of the thousands of eager eyes that were peering at him through half-closed blinds, and from behind curtains.   Still less conscious was he, I have no doubt, of the tenter-hooks on which his mysterious appearance had placed the good people of the vicinage.

When the announcement of the priest's arrival was first made certain by Josiah's oracular testimony, I could perceive that the Deacon glanced at me uneasily, and I purposely avoided his prying eye.   There were eyes, however, that I dreaded still more than his, a pair of dazzling orbs whose language I had learned to understand,—how, I could hardly say even to myself.   To these eyes, as usual, mine were irresistibly attracted, impelled, on the present occasion,

by a feeling that was far beyond curiosity. I expected
to encounter a fixed gaze full of malicious meaning,
and was prepared to look as defiant and as independent as possible. I had kept from looking at Eve
until the effort became painful, and with desperate resolution, I at last turned my eyes towards her
—and was relieved beyond expression. She *was* looking me full in the face, but in a way which I little
expected. She was evidently lost in thought, and
the expression of her face was such as I had never
seen it wear before. Dreamy, and soft, and subdued
it was, as though her thoughts were of a gentle,
pleasant kind, such as she loved to dwell upon. Meeting my eye she neither started nor blushed, but smiled
good-naturedly, I suppose at the sudden change which
she must have seen on my countenance. I could
hardly believe my eyes, and I know not what I should
have said in my utter amazement, but before I could
get out even a solitary interjection, the smile on Eve's
face had assumed its wonted archness, the softened,
pensive look had vanished from her eyes, and she
asked in her mocking way, " What *are* you thinking
of, Mr. Kerr !—ain't you going to take any tea this
evening ?"

Of course I was, and my apologies to Miss Olive,
when I found her hand outstretched with my share

of the precious beverage, were very sincere but very awkward, so much so, indeed, that Eve laughed outright, and even the evangelical features of her brother relaxed into a smile for which I could have knocked him down with right good will.

"Don't mind them, Mr. Kerr!" said Miss Olive with very unexpected kindness, "I reckon you were taken up, as I am myself, with the audacity of these agents of the man of sin. It is, indeed, deplorable; and calculated to make us think—that is, if we *can* think on any such serious subject," and she cast a vinegar-glance at her niece. The latter, in reply to the caustic insinuation and the petrifying look, shook her finger playfully at her aunt, and told her to beware lest she might be provoked to say what some people wouldn't like to hear. The ghost of a blush made its appearance on Aunt Olive's lank face, and she made a deprecating gesture to Eve that was meant to be seen by us all, as much as to say: "Don't now—there's a good girl—*don't* let out my little delicate secret!" There was an affectation of youthful bashfulness, too, in the spinster's keen eyes so affectedly cast down, that the effect was irresistibly comic, and the Deacon himself laughed as heartily as any of us youngsters, to the utter surprise and discomfiture of good Miss Olive. She had been playing off what

12*

she considered very pretty airs with a view to make
us men-folk understand that what "met the ear" was
little compared with what was "meant," and her
mortification was beyond expression when she found
the impression the very reverse of what she expected.
To the Deacon especially her anger was directed, and
after him Eve came under the lash.

"It ain't any wonder, Joel Samuels," said she,
drawing herself up, "to see your children miscon-
ducting themselves, when an aged man, like you, and
a Deacon, moreover, gives them such an example.   I
wonder at *you*, brother—indeed I do!"

"Why, Olive," said her brother in extenuation,
"flesh and blood couldn't stand it without laughing!"

"Stand what, Deacon Samuels?"

"Oh! you know well enough!—pooh! pooh! don't
be angry—what is it all but a joke!"

"Joke, indeed!" repeated the ancient fair one with
increasing asperity, "I know the joke it is—I do—it
ain't anything but real spite," and she darted a look
at Eve who was smiling and playing with her spoon
in the easiest way imaginable; "some people know
very well that they've lost the best string they had
to their bow—at least the one they fain *would* have.
Joke indeed!—we shall see how the joke will end!"
And so saying she sailed out of the room with the

nearest approach to the majestic that she could command.

"Why, do tell, Eve," said the Deacon, trying hard to compose his features, "why do tell what this means?"

Eve shook her head, but Josiah answered, "I guess *I* know, father; it's all along of Parson Greerson—"

Every eye was now turned on Eve, and to say the truth she looked somewhat fluttered, but still the careless smile was on her saucy lip.

"Parson Greerson," repeated her father slowly, "why, I thought—"

"You thought him a fool, father, but you find him a wise man—eh?" and with a piercing glance at me from under her long lashes, she tripped off after her aunt.

"Well!" said the Deacon, "it ain't any use trying to understand these girls—I thought it was quite another way—but it's best as it is, Josiah!—ain't it?" "Maybe so," was the answer, and so the matter rested for that time. I, of course, had nothing to say, but I felt puzzled and mystified, perhaps, somewhat glad, like the Deacon, but on different grounds for reasons to be shown hereafter.

CHAPTER IX.

ALL that night and the following day I could think of nothing but Parson Greerson, and his supposed attentions to Miss Olive Samuels. Do as I would, I could not get the matter out of my head, and I dwelt on it till my brain was giddy. Had I heard that the monument on Bunker Hill had been taking a sail on Massachusetts Bay, I could not have been more perplexed to account for its volition, than I was by the intimation of Greerson's proclivity to our ancient *femme de ménage*. Although sorely puzzled to account for his taste, I was fully aware that my heart throbbed and fluttered in a very strange manner at the thought that such *was* his

taste. Of all the male visitors who frequented the
Deacon's house, Parson Greerson was the very last
man whom I would have suspected of any such at-
traction, he was really a gentlemanly, handsome
young fellow, with as little of the Puritan about him
as I ever saw in any other native New Englander.
He was one of the most popular preachers of " our
kirk" in those parts, and, to do him justice, was master of a fine intellect and a happy vein of humor,
which, however, he was fain to repress within the
very narrowest bounds, in virtue of his standing
amongst "the chosen."   Now it seemed to me that
the young minister had been unusually mindful in
our regard of his duty of visiting his hearers, and
that principally since Eve's return.   It is true he paid
no particular attention to the fair daughter of the
house, on the contrary, he rather affected to avoid her,
but still I always had a misgiving that his eyes wandered in her direction oftener than they had any need
to do.   I had noticed him, at times, too, when con-
versing with the aunt, falling into a fit of abstraction
that to me was very suspicious, as his eyes followed
the graceful and fawn-like figure of the niece.   I had
even seen his whole face brighten into smiles at some
pert witticism of Eve's, until a glance at the serious
visage of Miss Olive recalled him to decent gravity

and a proper sense of his position. A new light had broken in on me through Eve's *badinage*, and the light was wonderfully cheering. But, alas! there was a cloud hanging over the matter—a cloud of doubt and misgiving that would not be dispelled, do as I might, so that fear and hope had alternate possession of my mind, and I was sensible of a nervous tremor, a flutter of anxiety such as I had never before experienced. Why all this, was the question I asked myself fifty times a day, but somehow I could never get a satisfactory answer from within.

Meanwhile the Catholics of the town and of its vicinity were making the most of the "days of grace" afforded them by the priest's visit. Almost the only one whom I knew for certain as "belonging to that persuasion," was an Irishman who worked by the day in the Deacon's garden. I know not how he came to suspect me of being his co-religionist, for, although I had many a chat with him about "the old country," I had carefully avoided even the slightest intimation of my being a Catholic, whereas Phil took good care that I should not remain in doubt on the subject of *his* belief.

On the Saturday evening of that week, Phil watched his opportunity (I believe he staid an hour past his time for the very purpose) and accosted me as I walked in the garden a few minutes after supper.

"There'll be Mass in the mornin' at John Gray's," said Phil, as I stopped to admire the neatness of a bush he was trimming.

"Well!" said I, with a start, "and what of that?"

"Oh! nothing at all," said he, with the queerest, drollest look, "only I thought, maybe, you might like to know. Among us *Catholics* here," and he laid a great stress on the word, "it's great news entirely. It's not often we've a chance of hearing Mass these times. Glory be to God, it's the fine opportunity we have now—if it 'id only last we'd be all right—but I hope there's a good time comin'. Howsomever, sir, if you're not what I took you for, there's no harm done."

"Oh! not at all, Phil," said I, with some hesitation, for I did not half like the comical expression of sly humor that was visible on Phil's nut-brown face. I was at first half inclined to confess the truth, but when once I noticed the quizzical look aforesaid, and fancied that Phil was making fun of me, and perhaps despised me in his heart, pride rose up in arms and obstinately closed my mouth on the secret. Still I would not appear to notice what was, after all, only a look and a half smile, so I bade the gardener "good-

evening " with as much composure as I could command, and strolled leisurely down a shady walk. I
was induced to look back more than once as I walked,
and, through the sun-lit foliage that skirted the walk,
I saw Phil leaning against a crabbed plum-tree, with
an unusually thoughtful look on his weather-worn
features. He was, doubtless, trying hard to solve
the knotty problem of my religious indifference.
Honest Phil Cullen! how sincere was my respect for
you at that moment, as you stood there in your mole-
skin jacket, your fine manly figure a personification
of sturdy independence, and your frank countenance
darkened with a frown at the thoughts of my pitiful
prevarication, which could not escape your native
shrewdness, aided by the light of faith. How poor,
how contemptible a creature was I in comparison !—
I, mean, truckling, shrinking like a guilty thing from
the suspicion of being a Catholic, which this humble
day-laborer doubtless considered his proudest distinction. Other thoughts crowded into my mind in this
connection—aye! thoughts of

"—— the mother that looked on my childhood,"

the pious mother who would cheerfully walk many a
long, long mile rather than miss hearing Mass on
Sunday or holiday. And the father who was little

less devout—and the sisters and brothers who were dwelling peacefully at home in the good, old-fashioned, homely sanctuary, where all virtue was inculcated, not by words, but by daily, hourly example—and the venerable pastor who had been so proud of my progress in religious instruction—all, all were before me, and my heart swelled almost to bursting with the multitude and magnitude of my emotions. I rushed back to open my mind to Phil, but Phil was no longer there. Happily, my dear-bought resolution did not vanish with him, and, as if in reward for the effort it had cost me, I was enabled to carry it out. So true it is that God assists those who labor in earnest to overcome themselves and their evil passions. The most serious difficulty which I had foreseen was unexpectedly removed by the absence of Eve, who had gone out to spend the evening, as I was told on entering the house. The witchery of her eyes once out of the way, I dreaded nothing during the evening, and had actually made up my mind to go to confession, as I knew the priest would be "hearing" till the night was far advanced. Now this I considered an achievement—I mean the resolution—and I felt myself more of a man during the hour or so that I had it before my mind than I had done since— since I came to New Haven. Avoiding all unneces-

13

sary conversation with the family, I retired to my
room soon after I went in from the garden, intending
to set about preparing myself for the solemn, and, at
all times, painful duty in which I was steadily re-
solved.   I had not been long thus engaged when rap,
rap, comes Josiah to my door.   What was wanting,
I asked.   Oh! somebody's grandmother had died,
and certain things were wanting that could only be
had in Deacon Samuels' store.   So down I had to go,
and when the store was seen open, sundry persons
popped in for something or another of which they
suddenly found themselves in need.   I was so vexed
that I could hardly speak a civil word to any of
them, but still they were all customers, and must be
served when once in.   By the time I got back to the
house, the Deacon was there, and Parson Greerson
was there, and some other notable individual with
him.   The Deacon could not hear of my going out.
I pleaded a pressing engagement.   It was no use,
out I could not get, unless I told the truth, and I
would as soon bite my tongue off as do that.   So
there went the opportunity in mercy given me, an
all through my pusillanimous fear of being known
for a Catholic.   I was on thorns all that evening, as,
indeed, I well deserved to be.

It was late when Miss Eve came home, so late that

I was already in my room preparing for bed. It is true it was only half-past ten, or thereabouts, but that was considered a late hour in the New Haven of that day. I opened my door softly, and stepped on tip-toe to the top of the staircase, so as to ascertain, if possible, who it was that saw Eve home. I listened anxiously, trying to catch the words that came dulled to my ear up two pairs of stairs, but I could distinguish nothing, save and except the parting " Good-night," which I fancied was spoken tenderly by Eve. Undoubtedly the young man's voice quivered in a way which it had no right to do, and I laid my head on my pillow to dream a harassing dream of the owner of that voice, a certain young merchant of the town who was esteemed a thriving man ; what was more alarming to me, he had long been paying attention to Eve, though with doubtful prospect of success.

After a night of feverish, broken slumber, I arose very early, and, profiting by the unbroken stillness of the house, stole softly down stairs and made my way to the street. I was determined to hear Mass that morning at all hazards, and bracing myself up, as best I could, for the probable or possible chances of discovery, I walked manfully on in the direction of John Grey's farm-house, which stood a little way

from the city, at the farther end of a pleasant green
lane, or what I would I have called in my boyish
days, a *boreen*. The house and everything about it
looked, it seemed to me, particularly snug and comfortable that bright autumn morning, with

" The corn-tops green and the meadows in their bloom,"

the richly-laden apple-trees in a small orchard at one
end of the house, and the soft, hazy-looking sun shining down with his gentlest light on all the pleasant
scene. But to me the chief beauty of the picture
was the stream of people, men, women and children,
that was flowing in through the white gateway, and
under the hop-covered door-porch. Oh! how my
heart swelled that moment with thoughts long unknown, unfelt. Memory was busy, busy weaving
her magic spell that carried me back to St. Kevin's
Glen and our new parish chapel, where the country-
folk, for miles around, were wont to assemble weekly,
in all weathers, to offer prayer and sacrifice, and hear
the familiar teachings of the good old pastor, who
had grown grey amongst them. When I, too, with
a lightsome heart, though, perchance, an empty pocket,
would

" Cross the fields to early mass,
And walk home with the neighbors "

My thoughts were sad, if not bitter, and I asked myself with a sinking heart, " What have you gained,
Simon Kerrigan, by leaving your old home ? have
you not lost more in one way than you gained in
another ?"

Before I had come to any conclusion on the subject
(other than the instinct which was the voice of conscience), I had reached the door and followed the
crowd into a large room on the first floor, where a
temporary altar had been fitted up, and before it in
silent prayer knelt the venerable priest in his white
surplus and stole. He had evidently been hearing
confessions, although it was yet but six o'clock. In
a few moments he stood up and commenced vesting
himself for Mass, while the people all knelt in pious
recollection. As I looked around upon the little congregation I recognized many whom I had never suspected of being Catholics, and others whom I did
know for what they were. Amongst the latter class
was Phil Cullen, whose round eyes were fixed on me,
as I entered, with a kind of half-pleased, half-mock-
ing expression.

During the time that the priest was preparing for
Mass I noticed one female coming in, whose appearance riveted my attention, it was so unlike any of
the others present. Her figure was small and grace

13*

ful, as I could see even through the long cloak in
which it was enveloped. Her face I could not see,
or even catch a glimpse of through the thick veil
which hung from her close straw bonnet. There was,
on the whole, an air of mystery about the figure that
attracted me with irresistible force, and I was almost
sorry when Mass commenced, because I had to turn
my back on it. I much fear that I derived little benefit from that Mass, good as my resolutions were as I
approached the house where it was said, for in spite
of myself my mind was wandering to the veiled fair
one near the door, and instead of reflecting on the dread
commemorative mysteries going on before me, I was
wondering who *she* could be, and to what Catholic
family in or about New Haven she could belong.

To complete my perturbation I fancied once or
twice that the eyes which I saw shining behind the
veil, like stars through a mist, were observing me
with fixed attention. It might be only imagination,
but whether or not, the effect was the same on me.
I was, as it were, in a fever of curiosity, and although
decency obliged me to face the altar, I paid no more
attention to the sacred rites than if they were celebrated a hundred miles away. I had made up my
mind to hurry out when the people stood up at the
last Gospel, so as to watch the motions of the fair *in*

cognita, instead of waiting to see the priest, according to my first intention.

I was doomed to be disappointed, however, for by the time I made my way to the door, the veiled figure was gone. I looked around in all directions, bewildered and amazed, but the object of my search was nowhere to be seen. A buggy was driving along the road in the direction of the town, but whether it contained the person in whom I was interested I had no means of knowing.

Slowly, very slowly, I plodded my way back to town, in a very different frame of mind from that in which I came. The sunshine was still bright on the fields and gardens, the air was still fresh and balmy, and laden with the thousand perfumes of fruit, and flower, and herb, the people were already dispersing, and wending their homeward way in picturesque groups, chatting pleasantly as they went. I alone was dull, lonely, and dejected, uncheered by the miles of nature, or the converse of my kind. And yet I could not tell why it was so. It could not be possible that baffled curiosity could alone produce such effects, but if not that, I could in no ways account for the depression into which I had so suddenly fallen.

The Sabbath amongst Puritans is ever a dreary

day—dull, and cold, and cheerless. The very cats
and dogs seem to feel the saddening influence of
over-strained and misapplied " religion," and neither
bark nor mew is heard as it is on working-days.   In
fact, cheerfulness (not to say mirth) is prohibited on
the evangelical Sabbath, so that a day which, amongst
Catholics, brings not only rest but joy, is strangely
enough converted by the people amongst whom my
lot was then cast, into a day of weary, dreary, cold
restraint.   Even the buoyant spirits of Eve Samuels
could not resist the overwhelming heaviness of the
domestic atmosphere, and although she laughed at
he hypocritical length of pious faces, and in her
neart had little sympathy with " the saints," still the
force of habit made her almost as grave and serious
on the Sunday as any other member of the family.

On this particular Sunday, I thought her even
more serious than the occasion required, and, being
myself in such low spirits, I felt sad and dejected,
longing for Monday to come, and with it business in
the store and the stir of life in the house, and Eve's
sportive gaiety, best and most effectual specific of all
to cure my despondency.

I would have given anything for a visit, no matter
who made it—except, indeed, it was Parson Greerson,
for notwithstanding Eve's raillery, and her aunt's

appropriation of his attentions and intentions to herself, I, somehow, could not get over my growing dis-
like of the man, based on fears which lay far down
in the depths of my heart. But no one came, not
even the minister, and we had to pass the day in unbroken stillness and monotony.

CHAPTER X.

THERE was a faint impression on my mind as I ascended to my chamber on that Sunday night that there was something unusual in Eve's manner, at least towards myself. It was not increased coldness, or keener irony, or yet any shade of bitterness, and yet assuredly the change was not for the better in my regard. In my waking moments during the night I had thought of it, and thought of it until I was lost in conjecture, and at last, towards morning, I fell into a sound, dreamless slumber on the conclusion that it was all imagination, and that it was only the Sunday cloud which hung heavier than usual on Eve's buoyant mind, which was sure to regain its lightness with the

cheerful dawn of Monday. After a hasty toilet I
descended to the garden, hoping yet somehow fearing
to find Eve there. Hope or fear, there she was, in
her broad-leafed straw-hat, and looking like a second
Flora as she bent over her flowers, watering-pot in
hand. Yielding to the strong impulse which urged
me on, I approached her. She must have been lost
in thought, for she started at the sound of my voice,
and I saw by the momentary glance she cast on me
that the interruption was anything but agreeable.
Anxious to know whether Eve was really changed,
or, if so, what had caused the change, I made an attempt to enter into conversation, but her answers
either came in monosyllables or came not at all, and,
with a heavy heart, I was forced to give in to the
conviction that Eve Samuels was no longer the same.
Not a trace remained of all that girlish coquetry,
that sprightly wit and drollery, which had so charmed
my senses. Oh! how much I would have given at
that moment for one of those sunny, flashing glances
which used to illumine the darkest recesses of my
heart. Even the mocking, scoffing tone which she
very often assumed in talking to me, would have
been now most welcome, but that was not vouchsafed
me. Hardly a word or look could I get from Eve.
no matter what subject I started, and I was about

to give it up in despair, when a desperate idea came into my head. Worse I could not be I saw plainly, so I said then what, at another time, I could not have got my tongue to utter.

"I suppose you're biting your nails now, Miss Samuels, that you let such a fine 'take' go off into your aunt's net!"

"Take!" she repeated, with a kindling eye, "what 'take' do you mean?"

"Why, the minister, to be sure!"

A scornful laugh, a bitter, scornful laugh escaped Eve, and she turned on me with the air of a wounded tigress: "Do you mean to say, Mr. Simon Kerr! that you can swallow such a story as that? I guess Greerson would be ill displeased with you if you believed it even for a moment. My aunt's net! Ruben Greerson in my aunt's net! ha! ha! ha!—no one living but a stupid Irishman would think of such a thing!"

I was nettled at the way in which she spoke of Irishmen in general: "As I told you before, Miss Samuels!" said I, "I am much beholden to you for your flattering opinion of 'Irishmen,' but Irish as I am, I didn't really swallow the story, as you say yourself. The mouthful was rather large for my throat, and wouldn't go down, do all I could."

" Indeed!—why, you astonish me, Mr. Kerr!—
so you are not *quite* so dull as I took you to be—you
are actually a shade or two in intelligence above the
nimal with the long ears so generally useful where
you came from."

Every word of this taunting speech went like a
dagger to my heart. A sudden faintness came over
me, and I was obliged to lean against a tree for support. The false spirit which had hitherto sustained
me was entirely gone, and I felt utterly miserable.

" This from *you*!" I said in a broken voice; "this
from *you*, Miss Eve! of all people!"

"And why not from *me*, pray?" and she turned
on me quickly with a lowering brow, but seeing me
leaning against the tree, doubtless as pale as a ghost,
her countenance changed, and she said in an altered
tone: " Why, what on earth is the matter with you,
Mr. Kerr? you look like a corpse!"

" Oh! it was only a little weakness I took," said I
with a forced smile, " if anything serious *did* ail me I
shouldn't like to have you see me."

"And why not?"

" Why, because I believe you incapable of human
pity—would to God that I had known it sooner!—
many a year of misery it might have saved me!—but
now—" I stopped, turned my eyes from her face,

14

and sighed deeply I heard my own sigh echoed near me, but surely the echo came not from the heart-less, heedless, teasing creature before me. Alas! it did, and more, too, much more than I ever dared expect. When I thought the girl so utterly un-worthy of real affection, she was most worthy, be-cause she was true to her own high heart, and spoke with a candor that in any other woman would have been set down as indecorous, perhaps imprudent.

"Look at me," said she, and her voice trembled; "look at me and say again that I am dead to human pity." I did look, and could hardly believe that the pale, agitated features, and the tear-dimmed eyes were those of the merry, laughing girl who had been for months' long the sunshine of our dull domicile. So great was my amazement that I could not speak. Eve smiled faintly and went on:

"I do not ask what you mean—I know it—I feel it here—" and she laid her hand on her heart, "I will not pretend to misunderstand you—a short time —a very short time ago I might have been—pleased —to know what I now know for the first time—but now—" she unconsciously ended in the same way I had done, but I noticed it not—I noticed nothing but the insinuation conveyed in her words, and that infused new life into every vein, and made my heart bound with renewed hope. I sprang towards her, and attempted to take both her hands, but she quickly placed them behind her back, and warned me with a dark scowl not to make so free.

"Come no nearer," said she sharply, "there is a gulf between us which neither can pass—you are in the condition of Dives, and I in that of Lazarus."

"How is that, Miss Samuels?"

"I tell you there has arisen between us an insuperable obstacle."

"Obstacle!—an insuperable obstacle!—why, what can it be?"

"That I keep to myself for the present—for you, I think you know it already—I *think* you do—hush! anyhow, there's father—not a word more—but hasten down that alley!"

For some days after this my mind was in a constant whirl of troubled thought. The sudden change in Eve's manner, the emotion she had betrayed in the garden, were each a source of anxious speculation. The latter might have given me a gleam of hope, but the former instantly obscured it, and left me plunged in the deepest gloom. I tried and tried to penetrate the mystery, but the more I tried, it became only the more inscrutable. And what made the matter worse, that wicked Eve plainly enjoyed my distress, for,

raising my eyes suddenly after a fit of painful musing, I often found her watching me with a singular
mixture of fun and sympathy that set my heart in a
flutter. To crown all, the old man appeared to have
been bitten by his whimsical daughter, for he, too,
was changed, and began to wax thoughtful on our
hands, and, as I considered, a little fretful, which,
to say the truth, had never been his fault heretofore.

Aunt Olive was just as usual, except that she began to entertain fears for my health, which annoyed
me not a little.   Often, when I was doing my best to
elude observation, and, perhaps, took refuge in a
corner from the piercing eyes of Eve, Miss Olive
would call out across the room : " I guess you're
going to have dyspepsy, Mr. Kerr! You look the
picture of it ! You must take something for it before it goes any farther. You must, indeed !"

Eve's mocking laugh was sure to follow : " I guess
you're about right, aunty ! poor Mr. Kerr had better
take some medicine—suppose you tried catnep, eh?
it's ever so good for the stomach, Mr. Kerr—it is,
indeed !"

I could with difficulty repress my tears, but I
managed to stammer out thanks for the well-meant,
though officious kindness of Miss Olive.

One evening when I felt, and I suppose looked

more depressed than usual, the good lady withdrew quietly from the room, and speedily returned with a bowl of—water-gruel, prepared, she said, by her own hand. Even Josiah's gravity was not proof against this, and he heartily joined in his sister's burst of merriment. I tried to decline the "gruel" with composure, assuring Miss Olive that there was noth ing the matter with me, and that I never could take gruel. She still persisted in pressing it upon me, till at last I fairly lost my temper, and bolted from the room, leaving Miss Olive standing on the floor with the unlucky bowl in her hand. Shrieks of laughter followed me even to the privacy of my little room, mingled with the angry voice of Olive; and, to escape, if possible, the unwelcome sounds, I threw myself on my bed, just as I was, and buried my head in the coverlit. That was a luckless night to me, for it cost me the friendship of good Miss Olive, who ever after treated me with coldness and that starched civility which was her general manner. I observed, too, that she talked very often, unusually often, of 'that dear man, Parson Greerson," pointing her emarks ever and anon with a glance of sovereign contempt at my unlucky self. Of course, I was much amused at the old lady's little affected airs, and, at another time, would have enjoyed them as capital

14*

fun. But I felt sick at heart, and could find no
enjoyment in anything, save watching Eve's ever-
changing features, and although there was little in
her eyes or in her face to cheer my drooping spirits,
I took a morbid pleasure in trying to read that fair,
but treacherous *index*, thence to form my conclusions,
whether correct or not.

So disturbed was my mind that I would gladly
have gone to confession had I still had the opportunity. But the priest was gone, and the hour of
grace had passed away, as I then sadly felt.

Things could not go on in this way. The Deacon
grew graver and more serious every day, and various
hints escaped Josiah that "father wan't pleased any
more with how I managed matters in the store."
At last the old man spoke to me himself, and fairly
told me that I wasn't what I used to be, and that
customers began to complain of my negligence and
inattention. "Now, once for all, Mr. Kerr," said he,
" that will not do," and he struck his stick on the
floor, " that ain't the way I made my business, and
what is more, it ain't the way that you got along
after you first came."

Had I followed the dictates of my own judgment,
or even of my own temper at the time, I would have
warned the old man that I meant to leave very soon,

but my heart failed me when I thought of Eve, and
I felt that, to tear myself away from the house where
she dwelt, would have been more than I could bear
Pride and prudence would alike have prompted m
to leave a place so fatal to my happiness, but prid
and prudence were silenced by the louder voice of
passion, luring me on with false, deceitful hope. So
I was fain to apologize to the Deacon, and in extenuation of my temporary negligence, meanly sheltered
myself under Miss Olive's mistake. I muttered something about the indifferent state of my health, but,
to my utter discomfiture, the grave old man only
shook his head and smiled a serious smile.

"Simon," said he, "I may as well tell you that I
have had some thoughts of taking you in as a part
ner—what would you think of that?"

I, of course, expressed my obligations, and said I
had no right to expect any such thing.

"Of course not, Simon, of course not, but I find
you so useful, in regard to your knowledge of the
business, and so good a salesman, moreover, that I
certainly thought of giving you an interest—of
course a small one, at first—in the business. I may
do it yet, Simon,—if—if—you will only pay attention
—and—why if there ain't our Eve, a-walking in the
garden with Parson Greerson? I wonder what he's

got to say to her—I hope he ain't a-making love to her, after all—for all she's my daughter, she ain't a fit wife for him.   She ain't !"

Away he stumped, leaving me still more agitated than before, yet quite willing to endorse the Deacon's opinion as regarded the matrimonial prospects of the pair before us.   I had an intuitive feeling that my all of happiness was staked on the result of that confer-ence, and my very temples throbbed with burning desire to know what I had to expect, or what to fear. I was strongly tempted to go into the garden, where I might possibly overhear something to enlighten me, but, whilst I was hesitating, I saw the Deacon make up to Greerson, and Eve breaking away from both with a laugh, whose ringing music reached me where I stood.   I knew not what to think, but one thing was certain. viz. : that I dared not venture out just then.

We had an early tea that evening, as the Deacon and his son had to go some miles out of town on business, expecting to return by the light of the young harvest moon.

After tea, I heard Miss Olive asking her niece to go with her to pay a visit to a sick relation, where-upon I betook myself to the garden, almost rejoicing in the excess of my loneliness.   I walked about for some time, thinking of the strange position in which I found myself, and wondering at the singular destiny which I fancied had brought me there, keeping my mind as far as possible from dwelling on its favorite object. All at once I remembered that I had received a letter from Ire and two days before, and had not as yet opened it, so entirely was I engrossed by the one thought. I had drawn it from my pocket, and was in the act of breaking the seal when in passing the arbor I involuntarily looked in ; and there, with her back towards me, sat the identical young lady whose appearance at Mass in John Gray's house had set my wits a-working ever since. I could hardly repress an exclamation of surprise, and my feet were as if riveted to the ground. The still unopened letter was again consigned to my pocket, and I stood with gaping eyes fixed on the graceful little figure which sat as motionless before me as though it were animated by no breath of life.

I know not how long I might have stood there, fearing to move, or to take my eyes off the mysterious figure, lest it should vanish from my sight like the *leprachaun* of Irish faery, but as it was I had not long to remain in such breathless suspense. The lady arose and turned towards me—the veil was thrown back, and the face of Eve Samuels was before me, looking somewhat as I had seen her for the last week, with the exception of an incipient smile which lurked about her mouth and eyes. Even this was encouragement for me and I made some steps towards her.

" Miss Samuels !" I exclaimed, " can I believe my eyes—"

" You can and may—how do you like my masquerade ?"

I made no answer—I knew not well *what* to say, so I remained silent.

" You noticed a change in me," said Eve, " and I *felt* the change myself. I could not appear the same towards you after seeing what I had seen. You now understand the why and wherefore—at least I hope so. It is true I do not feel at ease about the means which I took to satisfy my doubts concerning you. I feel that I did wrong in bending my knee with Papists in their idolatrous rites, but I tell you plainly, I suspected you, partly from some hints let fall by my father, partly from other causes—now—" she stopped, colored violently, and was preparing to move away. Her emotion was too visible, and too flattering for me to let her go so easily.

' Now," said I, repeating her own word, " in what is *now* different from *then ?*—you hated, you despised me before, what lower can I have fallen in your estimation—what is it to you, Eve Samuels! what religion I profess?"

I spoke bitterly, because I felt keenly, and Eve's trepidation increased with every word I uttered. "Hate!—despise!" she repeated, "who told you I hated or despised you, Simon Kerr? I am an American girl, and I never shrink from giving expression to my thoughts. I know *you* do not hate *me*," here she cast down her radiant eyes with the prettiest blush and the archest smile imaginable, "and just as little do *I* hate *you*—if I did, I would not have gone in amongst the children of Belial to watch over you."

"Watch over me!—how?"

"Why, because I am determined to save you—I will do it, come what may. You shall come forth from the abomination of desolation which abides in the Romish Church, or—or—"

"Or what?"

"Or either you or I must leave this house."

"But—but—" I hesitated and colored to the temples at the base suggestion which passion urged upon me, "but—suppose I—I—did as you desire (for my life I could not give a name to the foul thing which I then first saw as a possibility)—what good would it do me? Eve Samuels and I would be still as far apart as wealth and poverty could make us."

"You are mistaken, Simon," she said in a soft, yet earnest tone, and she moved a step nearer to me. How my heart throbbed at the sound of my own name pronounced by her for the first time. "You are mistaken, Simon!—I have reason to know that if you were a Protestant, you might have Deacon Samuels' daughter as well as a share of his business. I know not what you may think of me for speaking so, but I don't care—I tell the truth."

I hardly remember how I felt at that moment, or what I did, but I remember all too well that the flood of joy which rushed in upon my soul carried away all the barriers which faith or conscience would have opposed, and I said, almost without knowing what I did say:

"I will be whatever you wish, Eve Samuels! be mine, and make me what you please!"

CHAPTER XI.

I T were long to tell how I summoned courage to ask the Deacon's consent to my marrying his daughter; how he gave it, after some hesitation, partly, he said, in order to put Eve out of the way of his godly young friend, Parson Greerson, whose prospects in the Church would indubitably be injured, were he to form an alliance with an unregenerate maiden such as Eve Samuels; how Miss Olive was equally relieved by the unhoped-for appearance of the "Christian man" whose good offices she had so fervently evoked with regard to her wayward niece; how, in short, Eve and I resumed, and kept up to the last day of our single state, a constant Guerilla warfare of

15

sharp and pungent words, lying in wait for each other with exemplary patience, and darting out when least expected, with a charge of keen and caustic humor. Never was courtship like unto ours—at least I think so—since the days of Benedick and Beatrice, but, unlike that ever-memorable pair, when we quarrelled most in words, our hearts were the most attracted to each other, and our eyes contradicted what our tongues uttered. In fact, this continual whetting of our wits, gave a keener interest to what intercourse we had, and, I think, cemented our mutual affection. For my own part, I was so intoxicated with happiness, that I could not think, even if I would. But neither did I wish to reflect on the fearful sacrifice I was making—reflection, I thought, would drive me mad, or, at least, could only embitter my cup of bliss, the sweetness of which was now so delicious. What was religion with its unseen goods and remote promises, compared with the consciousness of being loved by Eve Samuels, and the immediate prospect of having her all my own? Bah! who cares for polemics, or theology, or any such stuff! To be the husband of Eve Samuels was the height of human blessedness, and for the superhuman enjoyments dimly held out by religion in an after life, I must only take chance. These were the ran-own thoughts wherewith I met and put to flight the promptings of my good angel, and before the wedding-day came round I had silenced them altogether. I exulted, of course, in my supposed victory, and gave full vent to the gushing flow of animal spirit which speedily bore me out of the reach of self reproach, and all other troublesome feelings of that kind.

At length the happy day arrived, and I received Eve Samuels from her father's hand. It was Parson Greerson who should have made us one, but it so happened that he was obliged to be in Hartford that day on very important business. Whether the business grew out of the occasion I cannot pretend to say, but I knew Eve and myself exchanged significant glances when the Parson's ceremonious "regrets" were conveyed to the Deacon in our presence on the previous evening. For my own part, (and I think Eve's, too,) I was not sorry that the young minister had contrived to hand over to a delegate what I felt would have been a painful duty for him The Deacon, Josiah, and Miss Olive were all grievously disappointed, especially the latter, whose new fawn-colored silk dress and beautiful chip hat, *a la* gipsy, went for nothing in his absence.

The marriage ceremony was hardly over when

conscience took up the lash and commenced the work of castigation which has hardly yet ceased, after years of remorse and sincere repentance. The friends and relations of my beautiful bride crowded around with their congratulations and good wishes, and my bosom swelled with rapture when I heard them salute Eve by my name, but alas! conscience whispered that the ceremony which made her mine in the eyes of the law was for me nothing more than a ceremony, and I shrank, as with a consciousness of guilt, from taking her to my bosom. "The law and her father have given her to me," said I, within myself, as I looked at her with swimming eyes, "but no priest has blessed our union—marriage is a sacrament divinely instituted, am I receiving it as such?—ah no! no!—our union cannot be blessed, for how even could I ask a blessing on it?"

Notwithstanding all my efforts, these intrusive thoughts threw a fearful gloom over "the joys of wedlock." Eve herself did not fail to notice it, and she called me to account in her sportive way for what she called my very unreasonable gravity. It was not hard to persuade her, however, that the cloud which rested on my brow was the natural regret of a son that the mother who fostered his infant years and the companions of his youthful sports should be so far, far away on his wedding-day. But the great day passed away with its tumultuous joys, its manifold recollections. Even its dark forebodings and sad misgivings came at last to an end, would that I might say, forever. But it was not so, such as that day was, were years of my after life. The golden vista of joy to which it seemed the portal was, indeed, mine during many a year of chequered life, but the remorse, the scruples, the fears and doubts which cast their gloom athwart the brightness of that day were only the foreshadows of things to come.

I found Eve all, and more than all, I had fondly believed her to be, and I never had reason to doubt that she loved me truly and lastingly. But unfortunately for my peace of mind, her sportive vivacity was in no way diminished by her assumption of the matronly character, and, as she had no great respect for religion herself, in any form, my change of religion was one of her favorite subjects of ridicule. It is true she had the good sense never to allude to it before strangers—even her aunt or Josiah never got a hint from her of my having once been a Catholic, but when we were alone together, or with only her father present, she indulged in all sorts of fun and mockery with regard to what she called my "cast.

15*

off religion." For a long time after our marriage, she never gave her father even a hint of her having been at Mass one morning, but once, in his hearing she forgot herself so far as to repeat in a mimicking way one of the Latin phrases she had heard on that occasion; her father instantly took her to task as to how or where she had heard such heathenish lingo. Poor Eve, unwilling to prevaricate, told the whole truth, and was severely chidden for her pains.

"I am thankful," said the Deacon with unmistakable sincerity, "that it is Simon's wife you are, rather than Parson Greerson's—a woman trained as you have been, in the religion of the Gospel, to enter a Popish Mass-house—"

"It wan't a Mass-house, father — there you're wrong," interrupted the incorrigible Eve.

"No matter, child! when the godless rites of Romanism were celebrated there, the house was accursed, together with all who assisted thereat."

This was too much even for me, and I asked the Deacon did he not believe that the Romanists worshipped the same God as he did.

"They pretend to, Simon—of course they do —but you know yourself they give far more honor to the Virgin Mary and their trumpery old Saints than they do to their Maker."

"I don't know any such thing, sir," I replied warmly; "Catholics, even the most simple, know well enough the difference between God and his creatures no matter how favored or how privileged they may be They adore but one God in three divine persons."

"Nonsense, Simon, don't we know they have as many gods and goddesses as they have saints and saintesses—han't they altars erected to them, and churches, and don't they offer sacrifice to them the same as they do to God ?"

"I tell you, sir, you know nothing at all about it—you just seem to know as much about Catholicity as you do about Buddhism—a great deal less, for all I know—and I suppose there ain't any sort of use in trying to set you right on the subject, or rather to open your eyes to the truth."

"No use whatever, Simon, I know more about Papist doings than I want to—it surprises me to hear you talk of them as you do—before you married Eve you didn't dare begin to talk so, and now when I thought you had turned away heart and soul from the unclean thing, I find you undertaking to prove it fair and spotless."

"But, father," said Eve, anticipating me, "it was you that began the subject, not Simon—you forget that."

"It don't matter which, Eve—if Kerr had really got religion, his sense of right—his conscience, in fact, wouldn't permit him to speak in favor of an institution which had its origin in the dark ages, and outlived them only by a diabolical miracle. Popery is a monstrous thing, an unnatural thing existing in this advanced age of the world. Faugh! don't talk to me about it—I ain't a-going to tolerate any man or woman in my house who has a leaning towards it."

"Why, Mr. Samuels," said I, more and more net tled as the old man waxed more angry, "why, Mr. Samuels, it's a pity you didn't tell me so when I came here first. You musn't have been so bitter against Papists then, sir, for I told you I was one."

"Yes, and you're one at heart still," said the Deacon with forced calmness, as he took up his hat and stick.

"Why, to be sure he is, father," said my riddle of a little wife, with one of her sly looks at me; "you might as well try your hand at that proverbially useless task of washing the blackamoor white, as to crub away the rust of Popery. The *Dominus Vobis-um* is in them to the back bone—eh, Simon?"

The strange quotation and its ludicrously wrong application tickled me so that I was forced to laugh.

"There now, father," said Eve exultingly as the

old man turned in surprise, " you see he's all right— you don't know how to manage him, that's all. Take my advice, and just say nothing to him, about relig- ion—leave that between him and me."

" Well! I guess you're about right, child!" said the Deacon.

" Of course I am, father!—ain't I, Simon?"

To be sure I answered in the affirmative, where- upon the Deacon nodded very graciously, and stumped away in tolerably good humor.

" Eve," said I, when we had the room to ourselves, " Protestants are much given to talking of Popish intolerance—ain't they?"

" Not more so than it deserves, I think," she re- plied gravely.

" What a pity they don't see their own faults as they see those of others—now there's your father, and if he ain't about as intolerant a man as—"

" As any Jesuit or inquisitor," laughed Eve.

" Or as any of your old New England Puritans," I retorted, " and they, I take it, were the most intoler- ant set of men that ever cursed the earth since the days of Nero and Dioclesian."

" Since the days of who?"

Instead of applying myself to give Eve a lesson in history, I set about soothing away the frown that was gradually contracting her finely-arched brows, and in order to do this I had to give the whole discussion the air of a jest, and assure her that I didn't care one straw about religion. It was only her father's tartness that provoked me to talk as I had done.

"He ought to be satisfied now," said I, "when I have abjured Popery to please—" I paused.

"Not him—but me—ain't it so?" said Eve with her arch smile.

"Exactly so—I made the sacrifice for your sake—and I would make it again to-morrow—but neither you nor any one else must expect me to do more than I can do. I have cast off Popery, as you call it, but no other religion will ever fit me so well—I can never get into Protestantism, whether Calvinism, Methodism, Baptistism—or any other *ism*. So just let me go on my own way, and I will give you no cause of complaint outwardly. I'll put on whatever religious garb you please, as far as going to church goes, but, for heaven's sake, let me alone about Popery—all of you. I'll be all the better Protestant for it, I assure you!"

The earnestness with which I spoke appeared to have its effect on Eve. Her love gave her the key to my feelings. Her lip trembled, and the color came and went on her peachy cheek, and her eyes were full of tears. It is needless to say that nothing more was said about religion then or for many a long day after.

The bitterness displayed by the Deacon on that occasion, however, made such an impression on my mind that I could not help thinking of it long and often. It was something so foreign to his real nature, as I supposed, and so unlike anything I had hitherto seen of him, that it puzzled me more than a little. I ventured once or twice to speak to Eve on the subject, but she only laughed it off, and said that it appeared I did not know before what a righteous man her father was.

"If there is any one thing on which he is more touchy than another," said she, "it is just as regards Popery. He hears and reads so much of its encroaching nature and its baneful effects on society that he both hates and fears it—that's the truth—it ain't palatable, ain't it ?"

And again she laughed and put forth all her witchery to banish the unpleasant subject from my mind. My own observations, together with what fell occasionally from the Deacon himself, speedily convinced me that the good man really did hate nothing except Popery. It was his weakness, Eve said, and she sup-

posed he couldn't help it. It was a harmless preju
dice, she thought, and even a safe one. For her own
part, although she was a little lax or so (that was
her weakness, she archly said), she knew how to
respect those who were always on the straight line
of Scriptural truth, and never gave way either to one
side or the other as much as a hair's-breadth. Whether Eve spoke in jest or earnest, I never could make
out—I rather think she was half serious, for I found
her out as time wore on to be much more in earnest
about religion than I had, at first, supposed.

In a continual tumult of this kind the first six
months of my married life passed away. I fancied
myself, notwithstanding, the happiest of men. I was
again in possession of the best chamber, with its
pleasant lattice opening on the garden, and I had re-
gained it under circumstances which, at the time I
lost it, I would have deemed beyond the range of
probability. The Deacon, at my marriage, had given
me a third of his business, so that I was already in a
fair way of making an independence. But above all,
and beyond all, I prized my wife, the brightest, dear-
est, liveliest little helpmate that ever was given to
mortal man, since Adam received his metamorphised
rib. Then there was the triumph over my formidable
clerical rival, not to speak of some half-dozen long-

faced young prigs, who, with all their pretensions to
extreme righteousness, admired Eve on the sly, and
would have bid for her hand (and fortune) had there
even been the shadow of a prospect of success. I
was acquainted with some of these myself and saw,
with unbounded satisfaction, what they would fain
have concealed, viz. : their spiteful chagrin at seeing
the richest prize in New Haven carried off before their
eyes by a comparative stranger. Their awkward
efforts to disguise their feelings were not a little
amusing, and this was especially the case with Greerson, who generally contrived to keep out of Eve's
way for some months after her marriage. This conduct was wholly inexplicable to Miss Olive, who was,
or appeared to be, wholly unsuspicious of the minister's real " proclivities." It was a matter of astonishment to her how he could keep away so long, and I
believe she never recovered from her amazement till
the enigma was solved by the handsome parson's
entering into a matrimonial partnership with the
young and wealthy daughter of another elder who
lived some miles from town on the Hartford road.
Who can tell the desolation, the despair which for
many days made the sere and yellow countenance of
my aunt-in-law a dreary blank to look upon, and oh !
the coquettish air of indifference which, by the end

16

of the first week, she succeeded in getting up. Poor Miss Olive! no wonder she felt this " the unkindest cut of all," for, at forty-four, a lover—even an imaginary one—is something both rare and valuable—something whose like may ne'er be seen again.

They were bright days those for me, and brighter still for Eve. The canker that has gnawed away the strength and vigor of my mind, and destroyed the best affections of my heart, had not yet assumed its most virulent form. I was happy to all appearance, and, in part, my happiness was real.

CHAPTER XII.

TEN years had past away since my marriage, and each one as it passed left some memento amongst us either of joy or grief. The Deacon had closed his eyes on this world just two years before, but not till he had seen three grand-children sporting around his knee. Another was born to us in the following year, so that we had " quite a family," as the phrase goes. Josiah and I were sharers in the business, but he had lately betaken himself to anoth er dwelling in company with a cer tain fat widow whose wealth was as noted in the neighborhood as her evangelical piety. Miss Olive was still, I might almost say, at the head of our establishment, for Eve was precisely of that disposi tion which rather shrinks from the multiplicity of household affairs, and gladly throws the responsibility of management on any one else. She had, moreover, a sort of liking for Aunt Olive, notwithstanding their frequent "spats," and knowing her to take both pride and pleasure in keeping the house which she had kept so long, she would not for the world attempt to curtail her authority in the least thing.

Had Miss Olive's watchful care extended only to our household affairs, I, too, would have been well content. Custom had reconciled me to the sight of her lank form rigid in perpendicular altitude at the head of our domestic board, ever amply furnished by her skill in the culinary art. Even the sound of her fife-like voice drilling "the help" in the kitchen betimes in the morning had become tolerable in the lapse of years, and, altogether, I rather relished her antiquated oddity of speech and manner. But there was one thing connected with her to which I never could, or never did become reconciled, for it touched me to the quick every day, every hour of my life, and kept the festering wounds of my soul ever open, ever fresh and bleeding. This was her Puritanical detestation of everything bearing upon Catholicity Eve was a sound Protestant, too, in her way, and could be as bitter as any one at times, but there was,

after all, nothing rancorous in her hostility to Catholics. She was opposed to their religion on principle,
but her hatred did not extend to themselves; she
could afford a good word even to a Catholic, and as
a Catholic, even for the discharge of his religious
obligations. Not so, oh! not so with Miss Olive.
Rabid and red-hot was ever and always her hatred
of "Romish people" and "Romish ways." It
seemed as though all the narrow bigotry of her old
Puritan father had descended in a stream to her. To
me the strangest thing of all was that she had never
come in contact with any Catholic, except, to be sure,
Phil Cullen, the gardener, and him she acknowledged
to be an honest, trustworthy man. Neither had she
learned anything of Catholicity from books, for her
reading was all on the opposition side, consisting of
ignorant and senseless tirades against a religion of
which the writers knew nothing. And yet Miss
Olive would have it that she knew all about "the
accursed thing," and her constant answer to any
word of extenuation in favor of Catholicity was:
"Don't tell me! I guess I know better!"

And there I had to listen for all those long, long
years to her perpetual abuse of Popery, and the num
berless tales she had to tell of priestly iniquity, and
Jesuitical intrigue, and Romish superstition. It was

16*

not my heart that hindered me from refuting the *
vile calumnies, which to hear made my blood boil
and my brain throb. But how could I, as a Protestant, undertake the defence of Romanism? Had I
been a real, sincere Protestant, with my disposition,
I might have been liberal enough to defend Catholics against charges which I knew to be false or
exaggerated, if only for the love of fair play, and
because they were absent. As it was, my own guilty
conscience and Eve's malicious eyes alike deterred
me from saying a word of all the thousand that my
heart dictated. I heard my own children, my boy
and my three girls, daily and hourly receiving instructions that poisoned their young minds, and filled
them with the most erroneous ideas regarding the
faith of my fathers, my own early faith, and the flush
of shame was on my cheek, not unmixed with indignation; but there I sat, with my eyes apparently
riveted on a newspaper although I saw not a word
of its contents. It had gone to my heart to see one
after one of the innocent creatures receiving Baptism
at the hands of a Protestant minister. This pang
soon past away, however, and the feverish unrest it
caused me soon subsided into the easy torpor of
indifference, which lasted till the next baptism came
round—births and baptisms were, of course, wholly

unconnected with us, for it was not till the child was able to use both limbs and tongue in their legitimate functions that the ceremony was gone through, such as it was. But the intervals between the baptisms were, unfortunately, not intervals of rest for me, owing to the causes before mentioned, and others not yet indicated to the reader.

Independent of Miss Olive's incessant, although aimless polemics, there were other secret sources of uneasiness, not to say wretchedness, growing out of my unhappy position. My poor mother's letters had latterly increased in frequency, and every one was more desponding than the other. All the money I sent her from time to time did not satisfy her in the least. She felt, doubtless, from tne tone of my letters, that my heart and soul were changed. The nature of the change, or its extent, she could not understand, but the unerring instinct of the mother's heart, aided by the light of faith—in her simple soul so serene and unclouded—made her feel ill at ease with regard to my spiritual state. She spoke ever of my brothers and sisters and the young families who were growing up around most of them, in that cheerful, hopeful way which was natural to her, but when she came to speak of my affairs and the dear children whom I took such delight in describing to her, I was bitterly sensible that her feelings towards us were not the same. In order to put her on her guard, I had told her, soon after my marriage, that my wife was a Protestant, and although she never sent me an angry word in reply, I saw all too plainly that the announcement had raised up a barrier between us—that my mother could never again feel towards me as she had done. After that she seldom mentioned priest, or chapel, or anything that was going on in regard to religion. By and by even "the patron" in the Valley passed off unnoticed, and this hurt me more than all, inasmuch as, every summer, since I left home, she had given me a minute detail of everything that had occurred there that she or the neighbors thought worthy of notice. These omissions touched my heart to its very core, and made me feel more wretched than I can now describe. The endearments of wife and children had no power to console me when I thought that the fondest of mothers had cast me from her heart. The good which we have not is ever more valuable in our eyes than that which we have, and the blessing whose possession gave us little or no sensible pleasure, is no sooner withdrawn from our grasp than we feel it almost a necessity of our being. Surrounded as I was by loving hearts, and loaded with the good

things of life, I yearned for the motherly voice and
the kindly smile of the old peasant woman far away
by the Avonmore's Banks, and I felt that I could
ave given worlds to hear her bless me once again.
But, alas! conscience was ever at hand with her
envenomed sting, and her icy whisper chilled my soul:
"Do you *merit* your mother's blessing? Are you
as deserving of her love, or God's love, as you were
when you left her straw-thatched cottage, to seek
and find a better home in the stranger's land?—think
what you were then, Simon, and what you are now,
and wonder not that even the mother who bore you
has grown cold and strange."

Starting from a reverie of this kind one day, I
found Eve's piercing eye fixed upon me with an inde-
finable expression of contempt, mingled, however,
with a certain softness which might indicate sympathy. I blushed, and she smiled—smiled in that peculiar way which no one else could imitate.

"What would you think, Simon, of a trip to Ireland?" she asked abruptly.

"To Ireland! why, what put that in your head?"

"Why, ain't it very natural for one to wish to
see what one hears a great deal about?—ain't it,
now?"

"But you have never heard much of Ireland."

" Haven't I, though ?—I guess I have."

" How ?—from whom ?"

" From *you*, and no other."

" Me !—me talk to you of Ireland !"

" Well! I don't say exactly that you talked to me,
but I heard you, which was all the same. Night
after night have I lain awake listening to the words
which you muttered in your troubled sleep ! Things
can I tell you, Simon, of which I never dreamed, but
which your disjointed night-ravings have made familiar to my ear as household words. Your old mother
in her drugget gown—(what sort of stuff *drugget*
may be I know not)—taking her fowl and eggs to
market—an old, old priest with silver-gray hair and
a certain Patricius O'Grady whose ferule seems to
have fixed itself in your memory—(disgraceful old
bears those schoolmasters of yours must have been !)
—and if I am not sufficiently well acquainted with
some old body called St. Kevin, and a queer, out-of-
the-way sort of place where he lives, or did live, it
ain't for want of hearing of him. Even the goats
that you used to be tending on some mountain-side,
I'm acquainted with them, too. So you see it ain't
any wonder that I should like to see so many strange
sights of which I am constantly hearing !"

My confusion increased with every word she ut

tered, and by the time she stopped (for w . of breath) I was fairly confounded, and knew n 't well what to say. Seeing, however, that Eve expected an answer, I stammered out something about regret ting her being so often disturbed by a habit which I never knew myself to have before.

"Ah Simon!" said my wife, standing up and lay ing her hand on my shoulder, "I'm afraid your mind is ill at ease. Your heart is not with *us*," and she looked with tearful eyes at our little ones, who were sporting on the green sward near us under the orchard trees. "Our religion is *not* yours,—there is a wall of brass between us."

What could I do but draw her to my bosom and assure her, as I did on that first fatal day, that relig ion was nothing—she and her love, all—all.

"Will you promise me, then, to struggle against these dangerous illusions—I mean recollections?"

"*How* dangerous?" I asked with rising warmth.

"*How!* why aren't they like the hankering of the Hebrews after the savory flesh-pots of Egypt? If your eyes were really opened to the light of truth, and your heart obedient to its voice, you would look back with disgust on the silly, and, I fear, wicked practices of a superstition which made your youth a dreary blank."

"Who *told* you it was a dreary blank?—I'm sure I never did. Poor I admit I was, and my lot lowly, but, Eve, it was not wretched, nor dreary, as you say—on the contrary, it was calm, peaceful, and—shall I say—*respectable?*"

"Yes, yes—out with it—why not?" said Eve with some asperity. "What a pity, Mr. Kerrigan, you ever left such a 'happy valley' as that sheep-walk, or or goat-walk, rather—especially as you can't carry it about with you like the old religion which you wear so slily under the decent garb of Protestantism—just like some of the lazy old friars I have read of who used to wear a hair-shirt next their skin."

"Why, Eve," I exclaimed, opening my eyes very wide, "is it you I hear talk so? If it was your aunt, now, I wouldn't mind, for I'm accustomed to hear *her* railing at Popery, and mind her talk no more than I do the rain pattering against the window when I'm snug within. But you—what's come over you, at all?"

"What's come over me, to be sure. Ain't it enough to drive one mad to see you so wrapt up in people and things near four thousand miles away, and making fools of us all here professing a religion that you have no faith in?—ain't it, now? I declare it does provoke me so, at times, that I—I—almost hate you, I do, *indeed*, Mr. Kerrigan!"

"Mr. Kerrigan," I repeated, "that's twice you have called me so since we have been speaking."

"And why not," she replied sharply; "where would my eyes be if I didn't know that your very name is a sham?"

"How is that?"

"How is it, you ask!—why, you great goose, how often have I seen your mother's letters—it is true you keep them pretty close, but still I have got sight of them oftener than you think. And the postmaster—don't you think *he* knows?"

"And did *he* tell you?"

"Oh! of course not," and she smiled with provoking archness; "he is a confidential friend of yours—ahem!—he merely *pointed* out the address to me, one day I was in there—he wouldn't give me the letter for you, having orders to leave your letters always till called for. Ah, Simon! Simon! hypocrisy and duplicity are, after all, hard to keep up! If I were you, I tell you what I'd do—I'd go back to Rome and get out some old *Dominus Vobiscum* or another—maybe St. Kevin from Ireland—to hear your confession, and deliver you of your spare change by way of praying your dead relations out of purgatory, and all that—or else—" she paused for a moment looked askance at me, and seeing that I had

17

no desire to interrupt her, went on rapidly : " Or else, Simon, I'd be in earnest what I appeared to be, and let not that great bond of union—a common faith—be wanting between you and your family."

" But it ain't wanting—what more can I do to prove myself a Protestant ?"

" Do !—why do what you do now, but do it in a different way, as though you were in earnest, which you ain't now !"

This was more than I could bear. The last pull which she gave the reins was too tight even for my craven spirit, and I began to hold up my head a very little.

" I'll tell you what it is, then, Eve ! I'm as much of a Protestant now as I ever can be. All the ministers in New England, with your aunt at their back, couldn't get me one step farther than you got me yourself at the very start. The fact is, I wouldn't listen to them at all, so they could never talk me into Protestantism, but you made me *feel*—you *looked* me into it, and in it now I am for good or ill !" I had worked myself up to a point of desperation, and I ended by catching her in my arms with an energy that was almost fierce, and, I believe, frightened her not a little. " I have accepted *your* theology, Eve ! I have staked my temporal and *eternal* happiness on

your love—I have given up—and for you—the my-
riad consolations of the Communion of Saints—but
don't be too exacting—you have lowered me to the
utmost in my own estimation—don't trample on me
now that you have me down—spare me, Eve, and
don't seek to pry into my miserable soul, let *its*
secrets be *my own*, and my heart shall be *yours*—
yours ever and only."

One of the children just then happened to fall, and
Eve broke away from my encircling arms, without a
word or even a look by which I could calculate the
effect of my almost involuntary appeal.

The reflections which followed when I found myself alone were anything but cheering to my lacer
ated heart. Here was I, shut out by my own suicidal
act from the communion of the church in whose doctrines my faith was as strong as ever, for, like the
devils, I believed and trembled. I would have long
since rid myself of what I considered the burden of
faith, and walked erect in the miserable freedom of
the unbeliever, but shake it off I could not. Night
and day it clung to me, and held my soul in its grasp
of iron, its fearful truths staring me in the face like
supernatural eyes of fire, burning and searing my
very brain. My days were days of dismal, hopeless
thought, and at night, even when sleep did weigh

down my eyelids, visions of terror too often thrilled my soul. To balance all this I had the love of Eve and the fair children she had given me. Alas! even that, even these pure affections were not what they ought to be, sources of unalloyed happiness. Every one of my children was a separate cause of excrutiating self-reproach. They were growing up not only in ignorance of true religion, but in bitter hostility to its divine doctrines, drinking in with every breath, the sour, acrid spirit of puritanical Protestantism, so diametrically opposed to the cheerful, genial, soul-enlivening faith in which I had grown to manhood. Oh! who can tell the torture of the thought that my apostacy affected not myself alone but every child I had, or might yet have, ah! and their children after them? This I had never taken into account until my children began to grow up around me, then it became one of the most deadly drops in the poisoned cup I had prepared for myself. Added to all this was now the thought that the wife for whose sake I had incurred such a fearful penalty, had no faith in me. "She sees me," thought I, "almost as I see myself, and how can she but despise me, traitor as I am to God and my own convictions. She sees me as a hypocrite, professing for worldly motives a religion which my soul abhors—I loathe, I detest myself—

how can she but do the same?—oh wealth!—oh.
wife!—oh children! how dearly have I purchased
you all, and yet you do not give me happiness—happiness!" I repeated with a low moan, " oh! there is
no more happiness for me! The God of Heaven
who created me is angry with me—the mother who
gave me birth is grown cold and strange, and those
who once knew and loved me, know or love me no
more—oh! would that I had never left the humble
shelter of my paternal roof! would that I had never
taken into my head the foolish notion of rising in the
world. Had I been contented in the lowly sphere
wherein I was born—had I been ' poor in spirit' in
my boyish days, I might now be cheerful and happy
as a summer bird!"

Just then the softened voice of Eve spoke at my
side, and her arm encircled my neck as she bent over
me where I sat on a garden-bench.

" The dew is falling, Simon!" she said very gently;
" had you not better come in?"

The voice and the words fell on my heart like
softest music, and the pressure of the little hand was
like the touch of an angel's wing. Hardly knowing
what I did, I arose and followed Eve into the house,
and the many-headed dragon took flight for that time.

CHAPTER XIII.

T HE opening intelligence of my children was to me, unlike other parents, an additional source of misery. As antagonism to Popery was the dominant characteristic of Miss Olive's mind, and my wife's views of religion, as far as they went, were ultra-Protestant, it may well be supposed that our little people learned to think and speak as they did who had the training of them. And I professing the same religion—no, not that exactly, either, for I could not have told if any one asked me, *what* I professed—*protesting*, at all events, as I appeared to do, against " the errors and corruptions of Rome," how could I dare to teach them anything " Romish," or even edge in a word on behalf of the much-belied doctrines and practices of that "persuasion." Had I been a real Protestant, "to the manor born," and free from the burning brand of apostacy, with even a slight knowledge of Catholics or their religion, I could have counteracted much of the pernicious teaching so lavishly bestowed on the children, but, endeavoring to appear what I was not, I labored under a continual restraint, fearing to be found out, and have my borrowed feathers shamefully torn off. And this fear was on me, not only in the presence of my wife, or her aunt, but even when alone with the children. If any of them made a mocking or contemptuous remark, as very often happened, in relation to some Catholic doctrine, seen by them through the distorted medium of their old aunt's bigotry, I was forced to gulp down my rising anger, and keep silence, or seem to laugh as they did, lest a dangerous report might be made to the ruling powers.

One day when I came suddenly on the youngsters at their sport, I found Joel, the eldest boy, entertaining his juniors with a fancy sketch of "the Pope of Rome," wherein that personage was described as having a cloven foot, stunted horns, and a most fiendish cast of countenance.

"Fie! fie, Joel!" I cried almost involuntarily, "what nonsense is 'hat? The Pope is just like any other man!—ain't you ashamed to talk like that?'

"Why, no, father!—its every word true—aunty says so."

"Oh! yes, father," put in little Olive, the youngest girl, "aunty tells us ever so many things about the big old Pope, with him horns and red eyes—and—oh! my, he naughty, wicked man—I so fraid of him!" and the child actually shuddered with fear and horror of the revolting image.

In vain did I put in a faint protest against the description of "Giant Pope." The impression was made on the ductile minds of the children by the oft-repeated nursery-tales of their evangelically-pious aunt, and as I dared not enter into any positive aescription of the Pontiff or his real abode, all I did venture to say, being merely denial, had little or no effect in removing the rooted aversion so sedulously fostered for weeks and months.

I took an early opportunity, however, of representing to Miss Olive the injurious effect of such tales of horror on the plastic minds of children. Miss Olive listened with a stony aspect, and when I had done, she turned on me with an eye of fire:

"So you don't like my portrait of the old fellow at Rome?"

" Well! it ain't—so much that—as—as—in short, you know as well as I do, or ought to know, Miss Samuels, that it ain't right to tell children such frightful stories. I wonder at a woman of your good sense to do it."

" Good sense—ah!—yes, I rather think I have a *small* share of that article—too much to have any leaning towards Rome—eh! *Mr. Kerrigan!*"

I started as though an adder had stung me. I looked at Eve, but Eve only smiled and shook her head. I looked once more at Miss Olive, and *she* smiled, too, in her grim, freezing way.

" Mr. Kerrigan!" I repeated.

" Mr. Kerrigan!" said Miss Olive after me, pro- nouncing every word so slowly and distinctly as to leave no mistake about it. " Did you suppose, now, that folks here were so very green that you could come it over them like that? Why, it wasn't many months after you told us ' your real name,' as you called it, till we found out your real, *real* one from Wilson Hunter of the Post-office. However that ain't what we were speaking of—you can still be *Mr. Kerr*, for all us, you know—but about the chil- dren. Don't you trouble about what stories I tell them. I guess you'll never hear of me telling them any that ain't moral and useful. If you think I ain't fit to assist Eve in bringing up her children, why just say so, and I shan't have anything more to do with *them*—or the housekeeping either."

The words that trembled on my lip were driven back into my tortured heart by an imploring look from Eve who took it upon herself to answer for me. She eagerly assured her aunt that I meant no harm, and that no one could be more sensible than I of the inestimable value of her care over the children, and her excellent moral training of them.

"Moral, Eve! you say moral only—I should hope it is religious as well—"

"Oh, certainly, aunt! no one can dispute that—in fact it is essentially religious," Eve added with a spice of her earlier archness.

I groaned in spirit as I inwardly assented to the truth of this half-satirical remark. Not so Miss Olive, who was so softened by Eve's adroit management that she even deigned to overlook my silence (for I had taken up a book), and asked me with rather more good-nature than she usually displayed on *any* occasion, whether I would not call Joel in to hear him read.

I assented as cheerfully as I could, and told the little fellow to choose what he should read.

"Oh yes, father, I'll read the pretty story mother

made me read this morning, about the great Romish
idols, made of wood and stone and all such things,
that they fall down and pray to. Ain't that horrid,
father?" said the child, as he placed his finger under
the first word to commence. Fain would I have
taken the book from him, and flung it in the fire
which burned so temptingly in the old-fashioned
brazen grate. But Eve's eye was on me, with more
than its usual significance, and, what was still worse,
Aunt Olive's eye was on me, looking awfully cold
and critical through the silver-mounted spectacles
which, of late, she had been driven by hard necessity
to wear. There was nothing for it, then, but to let
Joel go on with his precious lesson, and for full
twenty minutes I was compelled to sit listening to a
nonsensical and yet ingenious parallel between the
heathen gods of the Pantheon and the Saints
of the Roman calendar—the latter, it was said,
presiding over the spiritual darkness of modern
Rome as the former did over its pagan predeces-
sor. My heart swelled almost to bursting as I
thought of good St. Kevin, and all the beneficient
patrons of my childhood, whose guardian presence
threw such a charm around my lonely wanderings
in those happy, happy days when I was full of
faith and hope, and had boundless confidence in

the watchful care of those beatified servants of God.

"Alas! alas!" said I within myself, "this blessed connection with the unseen world, this all-consoling trust in the kindly intercession of the Saints, my children can never know—a dreary blank must their infancy be, deprived of this ineffable charm—oh misery! and am I to blame?—have I ruined them as well as myself?" Under the influence of this racking thought, I started to my feet, and telling Joel he had read enough for that time, I hastily left the house, nor stopped till I reached the river's bank where I threw myself under a tree to give free vent to the headlong torrent of bitter thought that was sweeping through my soul.

That evening, when I returned home, I found we had a guest for supper. He was a short, stubby little man with a bronzed, and yet ruddy complexion, enlivened by a pair of small, dark, never-resting eyes, expressive both of good humor and good nature. This individual had been in the habit of supplying the family with shoes, and although he was somewhat of a favorite with us all on account of his scrupulous honesty and imperturbably good temper, no one had ever dreamed of inviting him to our family table, for the truth was that we were rather fastidious in ov choice of company. Besides good Mr. Elliott had moved his business to the opposite extremity of the town, so that we had not so often seen him of late.

I was well pleased just then to see the man of leather at our board being nowise disposed to do the talking which I knew of old would be done by him in first-rate style, as to quantity.

" Why, Mr. Elliott ! I'm glad to see you !" I said, " its so long since I've had that pleasure—how goes trade these times ?"

" If you mean the shoe-trade, Mr. Kerr !" said the cheery little man, rubbing his hands as he eyed the tempting viands, sweetmeats, and so forth, to attack which we were just on the march, " if you mean the shoe-trade, I ain't in that line ar y more."

" Do you tell me so ?—there, take your seat near Mrs. Kerr—and what, may I ask, are you doing now ?"

" Preaching, my dear sir, preaching," and Elliott pulled up his shirt-collar, and affected an indifference of tone, in evident contradiction to the swelling importance of his manner.

" Preaching !" I involuntarily repeated ; " is it possible ?"

" Oh yes, sir, it's a fact. I've got a call from a congregation up Hartford side—a good one, too, I assure you."

"Oh! I've no doubt of that—but how—how did you get qualified—I mean how did your congregation come to know of your capability?"

"Why, as to that, sir," said the man of trade, with the slightest possible shade of pique in his manner, "if you were ever at any of our class-meetings, or prayer-meetings, you wouldn't need to ask that question. Miss Samuels there can tell you that I've been asked to conduct prayer-meetings farther away than where I'm called to now. I have had some little gifts in the way of prayer and expounding, too, for that matter, ever since—ever since Miss Samuels and I used to teach Sunday school together in Mr. Hopham's church."

Now the Mr. Hopham aforesaid had departed this life, as a handsome monument in his church-yard testified, just eight-and-twenty years before, and Miss Samuels, who was trying to look her best and youngest, was evidently little obliged for this gratuitous hint about her age. Still she kept her temper wonderfully, and gave willing testimony to "the gifts" before mentioned, together with her own private opinion that Mr. Elliott had been actually hiding his candle under a bushel so long as he gave up his valuable time to the covering of men, women, and children's pedal extremities. Hearing this Mr. Elliott

.ooked exultingly at me, and then greedily at a most appetizing plate of " dough-nuts " which stood near Miss Olive. The former look was responded to by a very sincere expression of satisfaction on my part, that the rhetorical powe's (I should have said *vocal*) of our friend Elliott had been at length appreciated ; in reply to the latter more expressive glance Miss Samuels presented the " dough-nuts."

Having masticated the savory morsel in a silence that was plainly luxurious, Mr. Elliott opened his eyes very wide, and fixed them on Miss Samuels, as though instinct directed him to the fabricator.

" I tell you them are awful good eating," said he, " did *you* make them, Miss Samuels ?"

Aunt Olive smiled and tried to blush, and Eve hastened to sb t 'or her what her peculiar modesty would not perm herself to say.

" Oh yes, Mr. Elliott, *all* our good things are made by Aunt Olive."

The new minister gave a grunt, whether of admiration or of satisfaction I could not make out. He was very taciturn during the remainder of the meal. and quite sententious in his answers when addressea. My wife and her aunt evidently respected the good man's change of manner, which they, no doubt, ascribed to the fullness of the spirit waking within him. To my attentive and more impartial eyes he was occupied with some weighty matter, requiring "nice con-sid-er-a-tion," as Sir Patrick O'Plenipo says in the play. Ever and anon he pursed out his lips in the peculiar fashion of fleshy men when they set about thinking; then he would heave a sigh—not your melancholy, discontented sigh, but one that denoted reflection; then he would cast a dreamy, half-conscious look over the well-covered table, and end with a glance of doubtful meaning at the unin viting countenance of my aunt-in-law. Immersed in thought as he was, Mr. Elliott took good care to leave nothing on the table untasted, and apparently he found all very much to his liking.

After supper, the minister took me one side, and told me, he had just been thinking that in his new position he would require a helpmate; not a young chit who might possibly give scandal by her love of dress, and even worse than that, but a sober, staid, God-fearing woman, who would enforce his preaching by her example—"

"And make good 'dough-nuts,' Mr. Elliott, eh?" and I smiled.

"Well, that too, Mr. Kerr, that too," and the minister's eyes twinkled.

"We're a-going to have lots of flour and butter

and all such matters sent to us—*of course*—and there
ain't anybody can care for things, or take such an interest in them as a man's wife. To preach well, Mr.
Kerr, a man wants to eat well, and to eat well a man
wants a good cook."

"To be sure, Mr. Elliott, to be sure. Now I think
I know one will answer you to a *t.* What would
you think of Miss Samuels there?"

I could hardly preserve my gravity, but the clerical gentleman was quite serious, and caught eagerly
at the word.

"That's just what I was coming to Mr. Kerr!
She's the very person—her appearance will make
folks respect us both, and her example will do good
among the hearers, I have no doubt. But, my dear
sir," he drew a step nearer, and took me by the
button, then raised himself on his toes, and whispered with thrilling emphasis that under the circumstances was quite pathetic. "But, my dear sir, will
the lady be agreeable?—I have nothing yet but the
call," slightly elevating his voice at the latter word.

In the fullness of my glad surprise, and the tumult
of newly awakened hope, I took it upon me to
answer for the "agreeableness" of Miss Olive, assuring Mr. Elliott, at the same time, that he might
depend on our best offices with our valuable relative.

18*

It is needless to say that the amiable and pious spinster was excellently well disposed to fill up the void so long existing in Mr. Elliott's side.   Whether it was the evangelically-soothing prospect of cooper ating with the gifted shoe-maker in doling out doctrine by word and work, or the economically gratifying one of having a larder supplied on such easy terms as Elliott described, she professed herself quite willing to undertake the twofold responsibility, nor shrank from the naming of an " early day," viz. that day week, being the one appointed for Mr Elliott's start.

I did not ask Eve, nor neither did she tell me how *she* felt during the week of preparation, and on the great day which saw chubby Mr. Elliott bear off his blooming bride and her wealth of five-and-forty years. For my own part I witnessed the departure of Aunt Olive without a single " drappie in my e'e," and indeed with sentiments of entire resignation.   I was very sincere, however, in my congratulations and good wishes, secretly hoping that the good-natured man of grease might find all and more than all th comfort he expected in his lady-love and her cookery, with which I, for one, was quite willing to dispense. Before she left our house, she was closeted with my wife for a longer time than I would have liked, and the nature of her parting communication may be inferred from the closing words which I chanced to overhear as the pair issued together from the back parlor :

"Above all, keep a close eye to the children—I have sowed good seed in their young minds, see to it, Eve, that it produces good fruit. Beware of Romish influences, my dear, for they are abroad, I tell you! Remember the blood that flows in your veins, and disgrace not the memory of your father by allowing his grand-children to stray from the way of righteousness."

The fruit of this "solemn injunction" was an increased strictness on the part of Eve in watching over her children's (supposed) spiritual welfare. Impressed with the responsibility of her position, she became quite religious on my hands, and unfortunately her watchful care was not confined to the children. I came in for my share of it, and henceforward every word and action of mine was scrutinized and taken note of for critical dissertation. Nothing could be more annoying than this change in Eve, whose lightness of heart and elasticity of mind were suddenly destroyed as by a crushing weight. All that superabundance of gaiety which had shed a charm over the darkest years of my life had vanished, as it

were, instantaneously, and the sprightly, witty little
Eve, more French than New Englandish in mind and
manner, all at once threw off her brilliant plumage
and appeared before my mortified and astonished
eyes in the leaden dullness of the paternal nature.
Sharp as fanatic zeal could make her, and peculiarly
exacting as regarded *my* religious views, because of
my Romish antecedents, Eve took upon herself the
office of inquisitor, and from that day forward, the
common inheritance of "free-will" was virtually a
dead letter for me. At least Eve would have made
it so, but the half-extinguished spirit of manhood
rose up in arms within me, and I assumed a defiant
and swaggering air which must have surprised my
wife quite as much as it grieved and pained her. It
was not that I ever went so far with my independence as to approach the assertion of my real convictions with regard to religion. That I would have
considered tantamount to disgrace, and pretty certain
of being followed by the loss of that position for
which I had sacrificed so much. With reckless desperation I clung to the outward form of Protestantism, which I still knew and felt to be a rotten shell.
Such as it was, however, I believed that it secured
me wealth and consideration amongst men, and for
that I prized it even when my heart and soul were

most deeply stamped with the burning brand of Catholicity scorching and withering with its fiery faith.

When the ominous struggle of which I have spoken was just at the highest, I received a letter from my eldest brother, enclosing a money letter which I had sent to my mother some two months before. My letter was unopened, and my cheek burned, and my heart throbbed as I turned to my brother's letter for explanation.

CHAPTER XIV.

Y brother's letter spoke in this wise:
"Mister Simon Kerrigan, I write you
these few lines, the last, I'm thinkin',
that you will ever get from me, barrin' God turns His hand with you, and
sure enough it's the back of His
hand He has to you now, any way.
Your mother sends you back your
letter—she doesn't know from Adam
what's in it, or what's not, but she
wouldn't touch a penny of your
money on any account. Her heart
was black with grief when she heard
of your marryin' a Prodestan, and ever since she had
no *grah* for takin' your money, but of late she got word
from some one in Boston that you had sold yourself
body and soul for the dirty dross of this world, and

from that day to this she wouldn't let one of us mention your name to her, and I'm sure all she cried
was enough to melt the eyes in her head. Don't
ever write another word to her, nor attempt to send
her money, unless you get out of the devil's grip,
for which she'll pray God, she says, every day and
hour of her life. But her days won't be long, I'm
thinkin' myself, for the crush that she got when she
heard of your turnin', she'll never get over in this
world. Nobody 'id ever know that they seen her
before, for her face is got the color of death, and her
eyes sunk back in her head, and she's bent a'most
two double. As you're doin' so well, you'll have all
the better luck for finishin' your good mother, the
kind, and lovin' mother that was a credit to us all,
and well thought of by rich and poor. But then, I
suppose, you got to be ashamed of her since you set
up for a gentleman, and took to the Prodestans.
Well, if you are ashamed of her, don't be tryin' to
heat the devil in the dark—leave her to us, and
we'll support her, plase the Lord! ay, and keep her
comfortable, too, which we're both able and willin'
to do. She's ashamed of you, anyhow, and not all
as one, she has good reason, for you have done what
not one of your breed, seed, or generation ever done,
and the oad of disgrace that's on her is too heavy

for her to bear. Only that charity binds her to pray for you as she would for any other sinner, she'd never let your name cross her lips, though it's hard enough for the mother to have to turn her face agin the child of her heart, but she bids me tell you that the enemy of God can be no child of hers, and them that could throw themselves overboard out of Peter's bark are out of her reach altogether. She'll pray God all her days that the fiery waves of hell may not swallow you up till you get the grace of bein' converted back again, and makin' your peace with God, and the Blessed Virgin Mother of Christ, and all the holy Saints and Angels that you've scandalized and insulted. As for Father O'Byrne, he can hardly believe it yet that you'd fall away from the true faith —he still hopes that we'll find it all a mistake, for he says he knows you better than any one livin', and he's full sure you could never be a Prodestan. Unless you can tell us that his reverence is in the right, you need never write a scrowl to us, for you'll get it back with postage to pay, and a word you'll never hear from one belongin' to you. I don't want to sign myself your brother, but I'm bound to remain your well-wisher, NICHOLAS KERRIGAN."

All the grief I had ever known was nothing to what I endured on reading this letter. Sorrow

shame, remorse, were for a while the alternate pos-
sessors of my unhappy soul, and at various times I
wished myself dead, little heeding the additional
guilt I thereby incurred in the sight of God. After
some time, my thoughts (if thoughts they were) took
a new turn. Pride asserted dominion over all the
other passions, and immediately the tumult of their
warfare was hushed into ominous silence. I all at
once found out that I was a badly-used man, that my
mother was after all neither more nor less than a
bigot, and hadn't the heart of a mother, or she
wouldn't be so severe on her own child. As for my
brother Nicholas and the rest of them, they had the
impudence of the Old Boy, and his ingratitude to
boot, or they wouldn't presume to speak to *me* in
such a way—to me who could buy them all from the
gallows—to me who had a carriage and pair, and servants to command, and the chief business of New
Haven in my hands, I'd have them to know I wouldn't
take any of *their* impudence, anyhow, and so I meant
to write to them, and so I did write, with the lauda-
ble intention of striking the iron while it was hot.
As for Father O'Byrne, I requested Nicholas to let
him know I *had* left the Romish Church, and felt all
the better for it. My hand trembled, and an ice-bolt
shot through my heart as I wrote the idle and desper-

ate bravado—the sign-manual of my own condemna
tion.   But pride and revenge—ay, revenge! were at
my elbow guiding the pen, and I wrote, at their dic-
tation, words of almost incoherent rage, for my soul
was in a whirl, and I took no time to consider what
I put down.   Fearing lest my resolution should fail
on reflection, I hastily sealed the precious epistle, and
walked as fast as my feet could carry me to the Post-
office, nor stopped till I saw the missive deposited
amongst the Boston letters on the official shelf.   I
strutted home in an ecstatic state of self-laudation,
and in the effervescence of my exultation, what should
I do but show Nicholas' letter to my wife, and repeated as nearly as I could what I had written to him
in reply, or as I termed it, how I had paid him off.
That was the unlucky revelation for me, for the peru-
sal of Nicholas' letter, and, indeed, the whole affair,
struck Eve as something so very ludicrous that all her
recently-acquired seriousness was not proof against it,
and she laughed as I had not seen or heard her laugh
for months' long.   Nor was the effect transient, for ever
after when she took it into her head to teaze me, she
was sure to fall back to " brother Nicholas' letter " for
a quotation, which she repeated in such grotesque
fashion that I had often to laugh myself when suffering most acutely from false shame and mortification.

This continued for months long, and then ceased only because the luckless letter assumed a lugubrious hue and acquired a sorrowful meaning from the intelligence—curtly and bitterly communicated—that my mother had at last sunk beneath her sorrows. This news sobered Eve completely, and I could see that she even reproached herself for having so often made free with the name of her who was now beyond the reach of praise, or ridicule, or censure. For me, I was utterly prostrated by the weight of a blow so unexpected. The loss of my mother would have been at any time a severe affliction, for, to say the truth, I always cherished at heart the memory of her virtues, and a grateful recollection of her tender care. But now—now when I could not but consider myself as, at least, accessory to her death, the flood of grief, swelled by the murky stream of remorse, overflowed every faculty of my being, and I was literally benumbed with accumulated anguish.

"The hand of God is on me," said I, "and I am but reaping the whirlwind where I sowed the storm. Still the punishment is too great for the offence. My sin is grievous, I know, but the penalty is dreadful. To kill my mother—oh, God! why was I born for such a fate?"

Thus it was that my hard, unregenerate heart,

although tortured with remorse, was as yet insensible to repentance, and instead of humbling myself before the outraged majesty of Heaven, I cried out and howled in impotent despair, accusing the God of all goodness, the God whom I had once loved as the kindest of fathers, of too great severity in my regard.

Had repentance then touched my soul, had I returned like the Prodigal in the Gospel, to the ever open arms of my Father, much after suffering might have been spared me, for the temporal punishment of my transgressions might not have been so heavy. But no, I persisted in the way my dogged pride suggested, resolutely closing my ear to the silvery accents of my better angel.

The death of my mother was only the prelude to a long series of misfortunes. My children, the pride of my heart, and the solace of my wretchedness, from being the healthiest in the town to all appearance, sickened one after the other and died of various diseases, until at last but one remained, Joel our eldest son, the first-born of the family. In him, then, all our hopes were centered, and as far as mind and person went, he gave fair promise. The boy inherited from his mother much of that fatal beauty which had won me from my God, and much too of the buoyant

spirits and sportive gaiety which came down to him
from his French grandame. These latter qualities,
together with a strong dash of Irish humor and a
warm, genial heart, would have made Joel a most
oveable character had he grown up under happier
auspices. But as his aunt well said, she had laid a
foundation of Puritanical ice down deep in Joel's
mind, and beneath it were buried the genial qualities,
the warm affections, and the generous sentiments
planted by nature in the boy's soul. Never was gem
so spoiled and defaced as my son's heart, and, like a
rare and cultivated vine on which a worthless wild
one is engrafted, the fruit of his advancing years was
bitter, and, alas! that I should say it, poisonous.
His mother and I made him our idol, especially after
the death of our other children, and truly, truly, he
became our curse.

With a natural disposition such as I have described,
and a training so pernicious, Joel grew up cold and
heartless—he had no religion in reality, but affected
a good deal. With all the precocious Teutonic
gravity which had distinguished his uncle Josiah at
the same age, he had a sub-strata of Celtic fire that
was ever smouldering beneath, and at intervals shoot-
ing upwards through the dark, marly surface in a
way that filled me with anxiety, the greater and the

more intolerable because I dared not give it utterance.   Eve, with all the partiality of a doting mother
for her only child, was still far from being insensible
to Joel's faults, although she gave him credit for
more religion, much more, than he really had.   She
would complain to me at times that Joel was wanting
in affection, and that there was something about him
she never could understand.   " He is so very silent,"
she would say, " and has such long fits of musing—
but then he is so pious, it must be the workings of
the Spirit that are going on within him.   He reflects
much, I think, on the things which appertain to
heaven."

It would have made me smile at any other time
to hear Eve talk in such wise (although of late years
she was, as I have said, quite a different person), but
this subject was too painful to me permit of mirth or
levity, and notwithstanding that I tried to reassure
Eve, my own heart was heavy with sad forebodings.

The first notable transgression of our unfortunate
son was the seduction of a pretty young American
girl, one of our " help," who went home to her
parents on account of her health, as it were.   We
afterwards learned that Joel had been supporting her
for some months, but finding the tax rather heavy
for his liking, he suddenly stopped the supplies and

declared against doing anything more. The consequence was that the whole was revealed to us by the
angry damsel. Joel was at the time on a visit to
Aunt Olive. We sent for him, and he came, but
instead of being ashamed, or touched by our agonized
reproaches, he laughed and answered us with a coarse
jest, justifying himself by the example of the older
patriarchs. As to the unhappy child that had been
born to him, he refused even to look at it. His
mother, however, seeing that he did not attempt to
deny his guilt, sent the forlorn creature to nurse, but
from that day till the day she died, no sound of
mirth escaped her wan lips, no smile beamed on her
wasted although still beautiful features. Had I had
my will the fellow should never have sat at my table
again, but his mother, with more forbearance, repre-
sented that by banishing him from our presence, we
might only make him desperate and lose all hold on
him for the time to come. The effect of *my* Catholic
training still clung to me, and although I gave in to
Eve's reasoning, I could not look at Joel for months
after without a feeling of disgust. This he was not
slow to discover, and he assumed, in consequence, a
brazen indifference that was still more offensive.
Sometimes when my temper could not brook his
saucy swaggering, I opened upon him in a vein of

bitter invective which, instead of doing good, roused the devil in his heart. The mocking laugh, the scathing taunt which scorched my very brain I was obliged to endure as best I might, for the least threat of punishment, the least appearance of passion on my part, brought on either a violent fit of crying or perhaps a fainting fit on that of his mother whose failing health and strength excited my tenderest sympathy. She had become so gentle, too, and so considerate, so grateful for any effort made to please her that, in the absence of any higher motive, it gave me, unspeakable pleasure to soothe and console her bruised and sorrowing heart. "She is worse than childless," would I say to myself, as I looked through my tears at her faded face, and her prematurely-bent form; "what on earth has she to console her, and what is there in *her* religious belief to give her solid hopes for hereafter? She talks like one in a dream of 'the Lord Jesus,' but I see, oh! too plainly, that His peace is not within her. Well! what can I do for her?—how could I begin to talk to her of the saving doctrines which would make her happy—I who have rejected, or appeared to reject them?—ah! wretch! the doom of your apostacy is on all you love, involving them in your destruction!"

One night, just when Eve had apparently reached

the last stage of weakness, I had lain awake most
of the night listening to her low, plaintive moans,
and watching, by the light of the flickering night-
lamp, the hectic flush that was burning on her hollow
cheek as she tossed about in the feverish slumber of
disease. Towards morning sleep overcame my fears
and sorrows, and I fell into a heavy slumber.

All at once my restless spirit was transported to
Glendalough, and by the grey light of early morning,
as it seemed to me, I looked down from the brow of
old Lugduff on the long-unseen but well-remembered
haunts of my boyish days. But alas! even in a
dream I was not as I had been in those fresh young
years. I was a man, and the crimes and sorrows of
my manhood were with me in that solitude. Op-
pressed by the weight of my " thick-coming fancies,"
and the awful stillness which reigned in the sacred
valley, I bowed my head between my hands and
wept. Suddenly an icy chill shot through my veins,
my hair stood on end, and a dreary consciousness
came over me that I was not alone—that I stood in
the presence of some disembodied spirit. By an
almost mechanical impulse I raised my head, and
there within two feet of me stood the sheeted form
of my mother, her ghastly eyes fixed full on me from
under the hood of her brown Carmelite death-habit.

I felt as though I could have sunk through the ground, and involuntarily moved a step or two away, but the figure moved after me and the power of motion suddenly left me. Speech, too, failed me, and there I stood face to face with the phantom, gazing into her soulless eyes, and feeling as though the marrow in my bones was withering away for fear. At last I sank on one knee, partly from exhaustion, and strove to articulate a question. The figure slowly raised her right hand and pointed to the large white cross on the front of her habit, then stretched her arm towards the opposite mountains. I turned and looked. Great God! how awful was the sight that met my eyes. High over the mountain-crest where the clouds had just cleared from before the blue sky, a fiery cross of immense proportions was distinctly visible.

" Merciful God !" I cried in anguish, " is this the day of wrath ?"

" Not yet," said a sepulchral voice from the motionless figure near me, " but by that cross you shall be judged. Wretched sinner, you have trampled on it —beware the vengeance of the man-God who died thereon ! Do penance, or you perish miserably."

" Mother ! mother !" I almost screamed, " what am I to do ?--can I ever hope for pardon ?"

• 'Ycu can," said the hollow voice, " repent and d●
p● ●ance, and your sins though red as scarlet shaL
become white as wool. But for a sign and in punish
ment of your apostacy, your idols of flesh shall be
broken and destroyed—so says the Lord of hosts !"

The oracular voice was silent, and before I could
muster courage to speak again, the unearthly visitor
had melted into thin air, and I was again alone with
the elements and the mighty hills.

I awoke with a start and found myself covered
with a cold sweat. I was trembling from head to
foot, and had hardly power to answer Eve who said
she had been some time trying in vain to rouse me
from what appeared to be a kind of fit.

" Oh ! Eve," said I, " I have had a horrible dream
too horrible to tell *you*."

" Alas, Simon !" said my wife with a sorrowful
shake of the head, " I fear that is nothing new. It
seems to me as though you never have any other but
horrible dreams."

" Why do you think so ?"

" Why, because I hear your strange mutterings
and see your convulsive twitchings. It does not
surprise me, however, considering that your heart is
as the barren rock. You are as a sparrow on the
house-top, Simon, far away from the Lord Jesus

whom you know but in name. I much fear that the chain of Romish superstition still enslaves your soul."

I answered only with a groan, for the vision of that awful cross was before me, and the warning voice of my dead mother was ringing like a knell in my ears. And thus it has been since, and thus it will remain, I fear, till my dying day—that sight of terror ever before my eyes, that sound of woe and malediction ever in my ears and in the deepest cells f my heart.

CHAPTER XV.

THAT fearful vision took such hold on my imagination that I could not get rid of it, do as I would. Terror had taken possession of all my faculties, and the fiery cross had impressed its image on my soul as with a red-hot brand. The bonds that chained me to earthly things seemed suddenly snapt asunder—all save the one that bound my heart to Eve. Rather, it was, that in that one tie all the others were absorbed, and I could in no way account for the fresh and strong impulse which my love for her had received of late. My son I could not love—my mother was dead—my brothers and sisters had cast me out from the family-circle. All this happened long before, and yet I was no more drawn to Eve than for the last few listless years I had been. How was it, then, that after that dreary night, when all other feeling and affections were, as it were, obliterated from my being, my heartstrings seemed to cling around *her* with a sort of tenacity and energy never known before. Ah! I could not see it then, in my half-pagan state, but now I see it as in a glass. It was yet another proof of God's scathing anger, yet another stroke of His divine justice, to increase the severity of my punishment and make it reach every fibre of my heart. In and through her had I sinned, in and through her was judgment to be executed on my guilty head.

About a month after that (to me) memorable night, we had a visit from Aunt Olive and her reverend partner, and as Eve had really, as I said before, a sort of affection for her aunt, her presence, together with the half-vulgar, half-clerical and most profuse chit-chat of good Mr. Elliott seemed to amuse and revive her more than a little. My spirits rose in proportion, and I felt the dreary load somewhat lightened on my heart. Even Aunt Olive herself was far less acrid than usual, and once or twice during the first day's dinner I actually saw her smile. As for Elliott he looked the very picture of good-nature, being on the best possible terms with himself and all

the world. I verily think that he would have cheerfully hob-a-nobbed with the Pope himself had he
appeared in his proper person on the opposite side of
the table with a quart decanter of fine old Port
standing on guard between. It was easy to see that
the good man's heart overflowed with the kindliest
feelings towards all mankind as he turned up his
cuffs, and whetted his knife for the great work of
dissecting a noble turkey which, with the concomi-
tant oyster-sauce, was placed before him. Oh! the
unction with which he pronounced his "grace," his
eyes taking in, the while, the rare proportions of the
savory bird before him.

Amid all the social warmth and unwonted cheerfulness which made our board a truly festive one that
day, Joel, our son, remained dull and silent. Gloomy
and morose he sat, taking no apparent interest in
what was going forward, but feeding like a ghole,
for his appetite was at all times remarkable. A sar-
donic smile played around his finely-curved mouth,
but it was evidently in connection with his own dark
imaginings. Many a sorrowful look was exchanged
between his mother and myself as we glanced
towards him, for I think I had never seen him look
more attractive than he did that day. His face was
of that transparent kind that reflects or expose

every passing emotion of the mind, and there was a fascination in his ever-changing features and in the occasional glance of his lustrous eyes that riveted attention, do as one would.

But still he persisted in his dogged silence, either vouchsafing no reply when any one spoke to him, or making some vague, half-conscious answer that was little less provoking than his silence. Every one noticed it, even Aunt Olive, whose favorite Joel had always been. For my part, I was so indignant that I could not wait till dinner was over to express my opinion of his conduct, especially as there were no strangers present. I had asked him a question without receiving any answer, and even his mother looked displeased at his contemptuous conduct.

" Did you hear me speak to you?" said I, raising my voice.

" No really, father!—what did you say ?"

" What I said is not of much consequence, but I want you to know that you must answer me when speak to you. Here have you been sitting like a statue since dinner commenced, hardly condescending to open your lips to any of us. I tell you once for all, Joel! I won't put up with such conduct, so make up your mind to mend your manners, or we'll see who is to be master in this house."

The blood rushed to Joel's face, and his eyes gleamed on me with a strange expression. " I guess my manners are as good as yours," said he, " do you think I'm going to be drilled and lectured by such as you ?"

" Joel! Joel!" cried his mother, " why do you speak so to your father ?"

" My father!" he repeated with bitter emphasis; " it's my misfortune that he *is* my father—"

" Leave the room," I shouted in a voice husky with rage.

" I won't leave the room," said my hopeful son; " you have no right to order me so in my grandfather's house!—it belongs to my mother and not to you!"

Joel and I had both risen, and we now stood glaring on each other with the fiercest anger. Aunt Olive and her husband each put in a remonstrance, the latter begging of me to keep my temper and the former reminding Joel that the disobedient child was accursed of God.

" Nonsense, aunt!" said Joel, turning fiercely on her; " don't talk to me of obedience to such a father as I've got—thanks to my mother's folly!—if there is a God—which ain't very clear to me—he don't require a fellow to be trampled under foot in a free

20*

country by an alien, and—" he stopped short and looked at me as though he feared to finish the sentence.

"And what?" I cried, roused to desperation; "what besides an alien?"

"Joel!" said his mother, in a faint but fearfully agitated tone, "be silent, I command you!—not a word as you love me!"

"He shall speak!" I cried in a choking voice, and I swore a dreadful oath; "he shall lay bare his black heart this moment. Speak, young man! what other foul name were you going to give me?"

"I think you know it yourself," said Joel, his face now pale as death; "if you *have* a conscience, ask *it*—"

"Name it you!" I almost shrieked; "what am I —a Papist?"

"Worse even than that—AN APOSTATE AND A HYPOCRITE!"

Maddened to hear my own son become my accuser, the words had scarcely passed his lips when I sprang on him and felled him to the ground with a blow of my clenched fist. The blood gushed from his mouth and nostrils, and he lay without sense or motion before me.

A wild, heart-rending scream burst from his mother.

She tried to rush towards him, but her strength failed her and she fell back pale and trembling in her chair, while Aunt Olive and Mr. Elliott raised Joel between them. I saw by their looks that they thought him dead, and yet with the stolid indifference of despair I threw myself into a seat and looked on as though nowise concerned.

This evidently shocked Eve yet more than the fatal blow. " Simon," said she in a voice of preter- natural energy considering her weakness, " Simon, do you know that you have killed your son—that the blood of your first-born is on your hand which shall henceforth be accursed of God and man !"

" I don't care—I couldn't be more accursed than I was. *An apostate and a hypocrite ?*—ha! ha! ha! The boy spoke the truth, but it wasn't for him to say it—he'll never say it again, anyhow !" and without another word or a glance at Joel I left the room, and ascending to my own chamber locked myself in. There I spent the remainder of the day in gloomy musings. Brooding over the dismal effects of my transgressions, and entirely absorbed in selfish sor- row that was not remorse, I neither heeded the lapse of time nor thought of the possible sufferings of others. It appeared to me more than probable that my unfortunate son had paid the penalty of his life

for his atrocious disobedience, but as yet the storm
of passion had not subsided, nor had repentance softened my heart in any degree; even the possible conse-
quences of my unnatural crime never crossed my
mind. An hour or so after I left the dinning-room a
gentle knock came to the door. It was repeated
again and again, and at last I was forced to ask
" Who's there ?" hoping to get rid of the intruder,
yet trembling in anticipation of the direful news I
might have to hear. I was answered by the soft
voice of Eve, begging for admission. Now most
people are glad and thankful to have some one to
condole and sympathize with them in their misery,
but not so me. I desired nothing else at that moment
but to be alone, and I felt as though the presence of
any one—but Eve of all people—would have been
insupportable. The sight of her pale reproachful
face would have been torture to me, now that I had
made her, in all probability, a childless mother.

" Eve !" said I, affecting a sternness which I did
not feel; " Eve ! I can't let you in. Tell me, however, is Joel dead ?"

" Oh, no—no, Simon ! it's not so bad as that—he
is ill, very ill, but not dead—oh ! not dead   The
doctor says he may live. Come and see him, won't
you ?"

"Not dead!" I repeated gruffly, endeavoring to conceal my satisfaction. "Well! it's dead he ought to be!"

"For shame, Simon! how can you hope to be forgiven if *you* forgive not? Come and see poor Joel!"

"Did he ask to see me?"

"No—but then his mind is wandering, you know!"

"Go away, Eve, and let me alone! go to your son —he's more to you than I am."

She still continued her expostulations, but all to no purpose. I spoke no more. At last she lost her patience and became angry. Words of bitterness escaped her lips which sank deep into my heart and made it hard as the granite rock. Within *my* soul was the dark, dogged, sullen spirit born of remorse and pride, and in Eve's, the stern determination inherited from her Puritan fathers, a quality which on ordinary occasions was but little perceptible.

"Do you forget," said she, "that that room was mine before it was yours?"

"No matter for that—it is mine now—I will not open it!"

"You will not?"

"No!—leave me alone, I want no companion in y misery."

There was no reply, and I knew that Eve was gone. "Now," said I to myself, "I know she has something in her head, for I never knew her to give way so easily when once her blood was up. I'll se what she is up to."

Strange to say, at that moment, my curiosity swallowed up all other feelings, and in order to gratify it, I unlocked the door, and leaving it wholly unfastened, stationed myself in the shadow of a large, old-fashioned clothes-press on the lobby.

I was not mistaken as to Eve's intentions, nor had I to wait long. She came again up the stairs with a feeble step, holding by the banister, and followed by poor Phil Cullen's successor in the garden, for Phil had gone the way of all flesh a few years before.

Peeping anxiously from my concealment, I saw that my wife was ghastly pale and that her whole frame trembled with emotion. My heart was touched at her appearance, and yet I was angry, very, very angry.

The remonstrative voice of Elliott now drew off my attention for a moment from Eve. "My dear Mrs. Kerr, take him gently," said the man of peace, as he reached the stairhead puffing and blowing after the ascent. "You know we have it in the Holy Book that a soft word turneth away wrath   Oh! don't—

don't now—let me speak to him before you do this
thing !"

Eve, wrapt up in the intensity of her own passion,
heeded not the friendly remonstrances, but made a
sign for the gardener to force the door. "But stop
a moment," said she, "perhaps it ain't locked now."
So saying she placed her shoulder to the door to try
it, and, leaning perhaps more heavily than she intended, from her weak state, the door went in, and
with a scream of terror Eve fell forward. In an
instant I had her in my arms, but she was quite
insensible, nay, to all appearance, dead. I carried
her in and laid her on her bed, and watched with the
most excruciating anxiety the effect of the various
restoratives applied by Aunt Olive and the women
from the kitchen. Elliott had taken his wife's place
at Joel's bedside to send her up to us, and to do the
old lady justice, there fell more tears from her eyes
over Eve's inanimate form than I had ever supposed
her capable of shedding. For me I retired into a
corner of the room, and watched the progress of the
various remedies. During the hour that my wife remained in that swoon I went through an age of suffering. I already fancied myself alone in the world, and
shrank into the depths of my wretched heart.

Who can paint my joy when, after an hour of

fruitless exertion, the vital spark manifested its presence in a long-drawn sigh and a convulsive twitching
of the limbs.   Eve was restored to life, but not,
alas! to consciousness.   The beautiful eyes opened
again, but the light of reason was not in them.   The
voice even made itself heard, but in low incoherent
mutterings, broken by sighs and moans.

That night I watched by Eve's bed, watched with
a never-closing eye, and a heart that scarcely beat.
I was alone with the unconscious sufferer, for Aunt
Olive watched by Joel, and others I would not admit,
even good Mr. Elliott, whose officious kindness and
trite homilies on resignation I dreaded of all things.
It was dreadful during those long, dreary hours, to
hear that low plaintive voice muttering complaints
and reproaches, which conscience could not fail to
apply to myself.   Occasionally she uttered the names
of her dead children, but of Joel she seldom spoke,
except once or twice when she charged me with his
death.

She had been lying quite still for some time, and I
thought she slept, when all at once she turned her
eyes on me with something approaching to recollection: "There's a curse on the family," she said with
startling energy, "and it's all along Simon's doing
I guess he'd better have kept as he was."

Independent of the fearful meaning of her words, I was terrified, for I saw some alarming change taking place, and I knew not what to do. I feared to leave the room to call assistance, which yet I desired with frantic eagerness. I threw open the door and called aloud for help, then raised Eve in my arms, and murmured words of endearment. It might have been that the familiar tones awoke her to consciousness for a brief moment, for she started, and her lip trembled as she looked at me again.

"You've done wrong, Simon!—to sell your God for a wife—and I did wrong to ask you—I see—I see it now—forgive—forgive me!"

Overjoyed to hear her speak rationally again, I forgot for the moment her perilous condition and tried to reassure her. A melancholy shake of the head was her only answer. She spoke no more on earth, and before many minutes had gone by—they were an age to me—I laid her down in her last sleep —a lump of breathless clay.

When Eve drew her last sigh it seemed as though the evil spell was broken that had so long held my soul in thrall. A load of sorrow weighed me down, selfish sorrow for her loss, but out of the darkness of my anguish came at last a ray of light. As I stood beside the lifeless body of her who had been all the world to me, an angel seemed to descend and trouble the pool of my overwhelming sorrow, and forth from it came repentance, true, genuine, Christian repentance, such as I had never experienced before at any period of my life.

As I looked upon the stark, rigid features that had been till late so mobile and expressive, and the eyes that were as liquid orbs of light now dark and dull and sightless, I said within myself: " Can that be Eve Samuels?—was it for that piece of flesh that I resigned my hopes of heaven?—forfeited the love of mother and kindred—and cut myself off, a rotten branch, from the tree of life? God of mercy, I am worse than dead in Thy sight—dead by my own act —a miserable suicide! What doth it profit a man to gain the whole world if he lose his own soul? Ay! what, indeed, doth it profit him? I gained the world—that is all I wanted, by my apostacy—what now remains of all, but some handfuls of the dross called money—money—ah! what can it do for me? Can it give me peace, or rest, or happiness, even *here?* Can it save me one hour from the final stroke that has cut *her* down?—oh, no! no! no!—one good confession, one act of real contrition, one deed of mortification, once to kneel at a Table which I dare not name, would do more to heal my lacerated heart

than all the wealth of London! Coarse and bitter
are the husks which I have eaten since I wandered
from my Father's house.   I will arise like the Prodigal and go back to my Father, for now I feel His
gracious goodness in this darkest hour of my life—He
beckons me from afar, holding out the Cross on which
His Son died for me! Ha! the Cross! it was to
crush my idols of flesh—it *has* crushed them—they are
utterly broken—the arm of vengeance has smitten
them for my sins—mercy! oh, Lord, mercy!—spare
my unhappy son—cut him not off in his wickedness
—punish me, but spare him!"

How long I remained in this mournful yet saving
lethargy of woe I cannot tell, but when Aunt Olive
towards morning came into the room, she found me
kneeling beside the bed, the clay-cold hand of my
dead wife locked in mine, and my eyes fixed in what
appeared to her a trance.

It was not till after Eve's interment that I con-
sented to see Joel, and I confess I entered his room
in rather a hopeful spirit, for Aunt Olive and her
husband had been trying to persuade me that he was
disposed to repent his undutiful conduct. Half an
hour's discourse with him unfortunately dispelled the
illusion. Dark and cynical and obdurate as ever, I
found him to be. He even upbraided me with being

accessory to his mother's death, and said, with a sneer, that I must be ever so much disappointed to find HIM in the way of doing well.

Smothering my anger as best I could, in obedience to the newly-awakened voice of religion, I strove to convince Joel of his error with regard to his mother's death and my feeling towards her. I told him I forgave him all, and even asked his pardon for all the suffering my unbridled passion had caused him. He laughed in my face, and asked did I think him so green as to believe all that stuff? This I could not bear, and telling him it would be long before I spoke to him again on any subject, I left the room and the house.

CONCLUSION.

A FEW weeks after Eve's death, while my good dispositions were still fresh and vivid, an opportunity was afforded me to be reconciled to God. A mission was again given in the town, and, although it cost me a fearful struggle, I resolutely prepared myself for confession, approached the sacred tribunal three or four times during the week, and finally had the happiness of receiving holy communion, after being publicly received back into the Church.

Great was the horror, and greater still the indignation of all New Haven, when it became known that Elder Kerr had gone bodily over to Rome. The whole town was in an uproar of indignant exclamation. Everybody talked to everybody about my miserable backsliding, and everybody told his or her

21*

neighbor that he or she never had faith in my princi-
ples. It was all at once found out that I had been
all along a suspicious character, and the only wonder
was that Deacon Samuels could have been so deceived
as to place confidence in me—above all to give me
his daughter.

When, on the day previous to his departure, I took
the priest home with me to dinner, the popular indignation reached its height. We were followed through
the street by an angry crowd of boys and women,
whose comments and apostrophes were anything but
complimentary. So long as they did not proceed
to actual violence, neither my companion nor myself
cared much. For my part, I was well content to be
reviled and abused, receiving it as my due, in a spirit
of penance. "I have been honored and looked up
to by these people," said I to myself, "in virtue of
my apostacy—it is retributive justice that I should
now receive all contumely at their hands."

All was well, however, till Joel heard of what was
going on. He was just able to walk about his room,
but as yet had not ventured to leave it. To my
great surprise he sent to ask me to visit him, and
when I did, he asked me very gravely if it was true
that a priest was in the house, and that I had gone
back to Rome.

" For the latter part of it," said he, " I am not at all surprised, but I won't stand it if you've brought a priest under this roof."

" It *is* true, then, but, even so, Joel, I don't well see how you can help yourself."

" I'll go down and kick him out !"

" Yourself shall be kicked out first. I'm master here, Joel ! and with God's help, I'll remain so, while I'm in it—which won't be long !"

" The shorter the better, for you're a disgrace to our family ! It's well for you and the Romish humbug down stairs that I'm not able to do what I'd wish to do—I guess I'd raise the town about you both and make it too hot to hold you !"

Had not divine grace enabled me to keep my temper there is no knowing what I might have done at the moment. As it was, I merely said, " God convert you, Joel !" and returned to my honored guest.

To think of continuing my business in New Haven with such a son and such a public prejudice against me was not to be thought of. I, therefore, made over the concern to Joel with the large stock then on hand, notifying him on paper that he had nothing more to expect from me, and that no further intercourse was to take place between us. To the latter clause he willingly agreed, impudently saying it was just what he wanted. As for "the concern" he didn't thank me any, he said, for it was his by right.

With a heavy heart I bade farewell to the graves of my wife and children, lingered a moment by the last resting-place of Deacon Samuels, and thought with many contending emotions of the luckless day when he lured me away from my Boston employers, I little dreaming at the time of the fearful abyss yawning before me. Still I felt no bitterness towards the old man, although he *was* accessory to my evil-doings, and I dropt a tear to his memory as I turned my back on his stately tomb. What I felt on taking my last look of Eve's fair name, illumined by the rays of the evening sun, it were useless all to tell, for who could sympathize with my heavy sorrow. Why lay bare to the gaze of strangers the torn and bleed-ing heart that was in my bosom? For that sorrow religion had no balm, for it was not only my own loss I mourned, but the scandal I had given my precious wife, and the probable loss of her soul, through my odious fault.

Her last words were ringing in my ears, like the voice of an accusing angel, and it was only the extra-ordinary fervor following on my conversion that kept me from falling into despair.

The last sigh was heaved, however, and the last

fond look taken, and I turned away from the spot
where I could have lingered forever. I had considerable investments in the Boston banks, and to that
ity I directed my steps. There for twenty years I
led an obscure and peaceful life,

> " The world forgetting, by the world forgot."

Most of my former acquaintances were either dead
or gone no one knew whither, and, on the whole, I
was glad of it. But even if any of them had seen
me they would not have recognized the handsome
and somewhat dandified young Irishman of their
former knowledge with the sallow-faced care-worn
old man—prematurely old—who showed little trace of
his origin in his outward appearance. During the
latter years of my Boston life, I had the happiness of
contributing a large sum to the erection of a Church
in New Haven, and the first priest who was sent
thither was the same who, so many years before, had
received me back into the Communion of the Church.

As for Joel, he soon contrived to get rid of the
business which had given a fortune to his grandfather
and to me likewise. He left New Haven and I lost
sight of him for some years until the time of the
Native riots, when, happening to be in Philadelphia
on a visit to a priest, I recognized my unhappy son

in a tall, brawny Hercules who was leading on the
mob in the infuriate attack on St. Augustine's Church.
Never shall I forget the demoniacal expression of his
once handsome features as he waved his arm and
called on the others to burn down the " Mass-house "
and clear the city of the rascally Irish. The sight
has never since left my eyes ; sleeping and waking it
is ever before me, and the thought of that hell-
inspired ruffian being *my son* is like a fiery dart stick·
ing for ever and ever in my heart. How I got away
from the window, whence I had seen Joel, I cannot
tell, but my heart was then and there made sick of a
country where such guilt and misery had been my
lot, and, I only waited to transfer my funded property to Dublin, then bade a final farewell to America,
and turned my face homewards to the dear old land
which in an evil hour I quitted.

Many changes have passed over the face of the
Green Isle since I left its rocky shores,—changes
public and changes private have taken place amongst
its people—the friends whom I loved and cherished
have passed away, ah ! every soul, so that, with the
aid of my altered appearance, I can pass myself off
for a stranger, yet there is something in the very
atmosphere which breathes of *home*. The warm
hearts and loving eyes that cheered my boyhood are

gone,—the *living* friends are lost to sight, and I miss
their enlivening presence, oh! how much!—but the
inanimate friends—the old, familiar scenes remain.   I
have taken up my abode in the very house of my
nativity—ruined, it is, and desolate, yet it is the shell
which contained the kernel of my affections.   The
fields are as green, the sky as changeful, the mountains as grand, the sacred valley as lone and solemn,
and, above all, the faith and piety of the people is
still the same, simple, earnest, nothing doubting, all-
performing.   Oh! I am not alone here, one cannot
be alone here, with the monuments of ages of faith
around, and the same faith ever living and acting
amongst the people.   I can go and kneel by the
graves of my parents and pray that my end may be
like theirs, and I feel that the penitent tears I shed
are acceptable to God, and that the spirits of those
over whose ashes I weep may one day welcome me
in glory when the last trace of my guilt is effaced by
whatever process God pleases.   Here, amid the solitude of the desert city, I meditate on the years I passed
in a foreign land, and rejoice that the feverish dream
is over.   Where I herded my goats, a peasant-boy, I
muse, an old and wrinkled man, on the path of life I
have trodden.   I stand at the opposite end of exist
ence, and ask myself what is the difference.   I have

had since what is called "position," I have wealth
still—ay! a fortune, but what of that?—I am old,
friendless, childless, and *alone*, burdened with harrow-
ing recollections, and ready to sink into the grave un-
honored and unknown. I was poor and unlearned in
those days which I now looked back on with regret,
but I had many hearts to love me; "now," said I
bitterly to myself. "I dare not breathe my name to
any hereabouts, for the memory of my crime is traditional amongst the people, and, did they recognize
me, all the wealth I have would not bribe them to look
with kindness on him who was once an APOSTATE!"

THE AMERICAN CATHOLIC TRADITION

An Arno Press Collection

Callahan, Nelson J., editor. **The Diary of Richard L. Burtsell, Priest of New York.** 1978

Curran, Robert Emmett. **Michael Augustine Corrigan and the Shaping of Conservative Catholicism in America, 1878-1902.** 1978

Ewens, Mary. **The Role of the Nun in Nineteenth-Century America** (Doctoral Thesis, The University of Minnesota, 1971). 1978

McNeal, Patricia F. **The American Catholic Peace Movement 1928-1972** (Doctoral Dissertation, Temple University, 1974). 1978

Meiring, Bernard Julius. **Educational Aspects of the Legislation of the Councils of Baltimore, 1829-1884** (Doctoral Dissertation, University of California, Berkeley, 1963). 1978

Murnion, Philip J., **The Catholic Priest and the Changing Structure of Pastoral Ministry, New York, 1920-1970** (Doctoral Dissertation, Columbia University, 1972). 1978

White, James A., **The Era of Good Intentions: A Survey of American Catholics' Writing Between the Years 1880-1915** (Doctoral Thesis, University of Notre Dame, 1957). 1978

Dyrud, Keith P., Michael Novak and Rudolph J. Vecoli, editors. **The Other Catholics.** 1978

Gleason, Philip, editor. **Documentary Reports on Early American Catholicism.** 1978

Bugg, Lelia Hardin, editor. **The People of Our Parish.** 1900

Cadden, John Paul. **The Historiography of the American Catholic Church: 1785-1943.** 1944

Caruso, Joseph. **The Priest.** 1956

Congress of Colored Catholics of the United States. **Three Catholic Afro-American Congresses.** [1893]

Day, Dorothy. **From Union Square to Rome.** 1940

Deshon, George. **Guide for Catholic Young Women.** 1897

Dorsey, Anna H[anson]. **The Flemmings.** [1869]

Egan, Maurice Francis. **The Disappearance of John Longworthy.** 1890

Ellard, Gerald. **Christian Life and Worship.** 1948

England, John. **The Works of the Right Rev. John England, First Bishop of Charleston.** 1849. 5 vols.

Fichter, Joseph H. **Dynamics of a City Church.** 1951

Furfey, Paul Hanly. **Fire on the Earth.** 1936

Garraghan, Gilbert J. **The Jesuits of the Middle United States.** 1938. 3 vols.

Gibbons, James. **The Faith of Our Fathers.** 1877

Hecker, I[saac] T[homas]. **Questions of the Soul.** 1855

Houtart, François. **Aspects Sociologiques Du Catholicisme Américain.** 1957

[Hughes, William H.] **Souvenir Volume. Three Great Events in the History of the Catholic Church in the United States.** 1889

[Huntington, Jedediah Vincent]. **Alban: A Tale of the New World.** 1851

Kelley, Francis C., editor. The First American Catholic Missionary Congress. 1909

Labbé, Dolores Egger. **Jim Crow Comes to Church.** 1971

LaFarge, John. **Interracial Justice.** 1937

Malone, Sylvester L. **Dr. Edward McGlynn.** 1918

The Mission-Book of the Congregation of the Most Holy Redeemer. 1862

O'Hara, Edwin V. **The Church and the Country Community.** 1927

Pise, Charles Constantine. **Father Rowland.** 1829

Ryan, Alvan S., editor. **The Brownson Reader.** 1955

Ryan, John A., **Distributive Justice.** 1916

Sadlier, [Mary Anne]. **Confessions of an Apostate.** 1903

Sermons Preached at the Church of St. Paul the Apostle, New York, During the Year 1863. 1864

Shea, John Gilmary. **A History of the Catholic Church Within the Limits of the United States.** 1886/1888/1890/1892. 4 Vols.

Shuster, George N. **The Catholic Spirit in America.** 1928

Spalding, J[ohn] L[ancaster]. **The Religious Mission of the Irish People and Catholic Colonization.** 1880

Sullivan, Richard. **Summer After Summer.** 1942

[Sullivan, William L.] **The Priest.** 1911

Thorp, Willard. **Catholic Novelists in Defense of Their Faith, 1829-1865.** 1968

Tincker, Mary Agnes. **San Salvador.** 1892

Weninger, Franz Xaver. **Die Heilige Mission** *and* **Praktische Winke Für Missionare.** 1885. 2 Vols. in 1

Wissel, Joseph. **The Redemptorist on the American Missions.** 1920. 3 Vols. in 2

The World's Columbian Catholic Congresses and Educational Exhibit. 1893

Zahm, J[ohn] A[ugustine]. **Evolution and Dogma.** 1896